Ghost
of Ian
Stanley

The Ghosts of Ian Stanley

I

Grace and Thomas Lockhaven

TWISTED KEY
publishing

2019

First Printing: 2019

ISBN 978-1-947744-44-8

Twisted Key Publishing, LLC
www.twistedkeypublishing.com

Ordering Information:
Special discounts are available on quantity purchases by corporations, associations, educators, and others. For details, contact the publisher at the above listed address.

U.S. trade bookstores and wholesalers: Please contact Twisted Key Publishing, LLC by email twistedkeypublishing@gmail.com.

Dedication

To my parents, Robin and Ivette, who were always there for me when I felt frightened in the middle of the night. No matter the hour, you would each scooch to opposite sides of the bed, so I could climb into the middle and sleep, feeling safe and protected.

Grace Lockhaven

Contents

Chapter 1

My name's Ian Stanley and I see dead people. Unfortunately, only the evil ones.... Sigh.... They say the vilest things that I wish I could remove from my memory.

You see, I'm only 12 years old, but I know as much as adults know...maybe more. I'm what adults call precocious or gifted. I guess the dead are obsessed with me, because it makes them feel connected to the world of the living. Just great....

I grew up to be the odd child in the family. How was I supposed to know that seeing people they couldn't see was abnormal? I thought translucent just meant they were incredibly pale, or vegan.

Madison, who's been my classmate for a couple of years, is the only one who believes me, but she's weird and annoying. She likes to call me special, but I insist I'm doomed...for life.

I have multiple ghosts bothering me every single day nonstop. They are the most irritating, most obnoxious people that had ever lived on the face of this planet. ~~It's no wonder they're all dead.~~

I don't tell Madison much about them just because I don't want to give her any satisfaction. She's just as irritating and obnoxious as they are, ~~but...she's still very much alive.~~

Besides, I don't see the point of being able to see evil spirits. They're completely worthless. It would've been great if I could see the good ones. I used to get so excited to go to funerals to be able to see the people I cared about again. I would wait and wait, but nothing would happen. They would never appear. They were just...gone.

Everyone thought I was cold-hearted for not crying at the funerals, they wondered how I could be cheerful at such a sad time. I hadn't realized yet, that they were truly gone.

It was terribly confusing. You see, the good people, when they die, they go to a better place, and they're gone forever. I was horribly depressed when I couldn't see them anymore...but also relieved when I finally understood that they weren't stuck in hell, purgatory, or whatever you call being stuck on Earth.

I wish I could meet someone else who can see ghosts, but not even these useless crooks have met anyone like me. I don't know if I'm the only one in the world that can communicate with them; it would be ridiculous if I was. It's not that I would want something in common with someone, I just want to know if anyone knows how to get rid of them and—

"IAN!"

Frustrated, Ian slammed the pencil on his desk, pulled off his headphones and yelled back at Xavier the Slicer. "WHAT?!"

Xavier smiled, finally grabbing Ian's attention. Xavier was the only one Ian had seen wearing military clothing from the 1700s. His dark blue coat rested over a buttoned-down beige waistcoat. A white steinkirk adorned his neck, the loose ends reaching the top of his belly. His dark red breeches ran down his knee, connecting to his white stockings, which tucked into his black shoes. His long hair was pulled back in a braided ponytail. He had a ginormous pig-nose, eyes wide and wild, and thin lips that accentuated his disturbing crooked teeth. "I've been trying to talk to you for the past hour!" he complained. "What are you writing about that's *so* important you had the audacity to ignore me?"

"I'm writing about you," he replied in a dull voice.

"Oh, well I didn't realize how special I was to you." He rubbed the loose ends of his steinkirk between his fingers, enjoying the moment. "My very own biography. If you're going to write about me, don't leave out any of the details of how I *preyed* on my victims." His eyes turned upwards; Ian was sure he was reminiscing about a past escapade.

"Don't be so flattered," warned Ian, "it's about wanting to get rid of you for good."

Sneaky Helga burst out laughing. "Feeling special now?" she scoffed, in her hoarse voice. Despite the fact that she wore a knee-length, loose-fitting red dress, you could see her entire body rippling beneath it. The low neckline made it easy to see her double chin trembling, almost swallowing her pearl necklace with every movement.

Xavier turned angrily on Helga narrowing his eyes: "Fatty! You think you're so funny. I promise you, that if we're ever reincarnated, I'm carving you up first." His mouth turned upward in an evil smile as he relished the thought.

"Ooooo, so scared," Helga laughed shaking her hands at him.

Ian shook his head, put the headphones back on and began writing again in his diary.

"IAN STOOOP!" Xavier exclaimed.

Ian angrily threw his headphones to the floor and screamed: "Say what you're going to say and be done with it!"

"I want to know if you're going to help me find my killer or not!" demanded Xavier.

"Ignoring you means no," hissed Ian, exasperated.

"Well let me help you regret ignoring me then," he leaned in closer, his lips nearly touching Ian's ear. "I can tell you where some treasure is if you help me," he whispered with a smug face.

"I don't care."

"Like hell you don't!" his hands balling up into fists. "This treasure is worth millions and it took me forever to find it."

"I'm glad you wasted your time, go find another human that cares."

Xavier floated back onto his heels. The reality of Ian's words, impaling him like a knife.

"What do you want then?! If it's not money, what is it?!" his voice a mixture of annoyance and desperation.

"For all of you to go away and *never* come back," Ian responded flatly.

"Well, you know I'm not going to do that, so you're going to have to make another wish," Xavier smiled, crossing his arms defiantly.

"Why are you so obsessed with finding the person that killed you? There's absolutely *nothing* you can do about it," interjected Helga.

"He's dead and he's here somewhere," said Xavier, turning his head from side to side, as if the person was suddenly going to appear in the room. "When I find him...," he rubbed his hands together, "let's just say I'm going to make his death a living hell."

"By yelling at him?" scoffed an aloof voice. Peter the Lecher had joined in on the foray.

Ian moaned, dropping his head on his hands. Peter never cared much about what happened around him unless it was about him. He tended to speak in a sophisticated manner, which Ian thought matched his outfit. He wore a top hat and had a bushy mustache that curled upward at both ends. He said they grew that way naturally, but Ian had a suspicion that he waxed them.

His black tailcoat sat over a white vest, adorned with a small black bow tie. His trousers were also black, striped vertically with thin gray lines, that accentuated his black silky Opera Pumps.

"I'll annoy the hell out of him for as long as I can. R.I.P my butt, it's going to be R.I.H. He's going to regret ever killing me." At that, Xavier came up with an idea and turned to Ian. "Kid, if you help me find my murderer, I promise I'll *never* bother you again. There would be no need," he said, shrugging his shoulders. "I would have found my purpose in death." He looked around at the other ghosts for their support.

Even though Ian would have eaten chopped liver and pickled pig feet for a year to get rid of Xavier, he knew that they were compulsive liars. He knew, they would always come back. Ian grabbed his pencil and began writing again.

"Are you ignoring me?!" Xavier yelled.

"Yes. I know that they only had a remedial education system in the 1700's, but surely you understand what ignoring someone means," Ian smiled.

Everyone jumped as Ian's bedroom door flew open. "Are you talking to your imaginary friends again or to yourself?" It was his 8-year-old sister Amy. Her uninterested expression suggested it was more of a statement than a question.

"Learn to knock first!" Ian snapped.

She stared at Ian with a tilt of her head and bored gray eyes. Her bangs fell over her curved eyebrows, making her look deceivingly angelic. She was dressed in her favorite lime-green sweatshirt, with the hood over her head, covering her long straight light brown hair. If it weren't for her black leggings and purple boots, she could almost pass as a boy. "Why? Are you embarrassed?"

"What do you want?" muttered Ian, glaring at his sister.

"Mom's been calling you. Dinner's ready," she said, slamming the door as she walked away.

Peter had waited until there was a moment of silence, before he began babbling in a poetic manner, "Ian, my dear boy, you should've seen how *beautiful* Melody looked today—"

Ian stood up from his chair, opened his bedroom door, and walked out, slamming it behind him.

Chapter 2

The smell of Ian's favorite food wafted up the stairs. Usually, this would put him in a better mood, but the site of Ronald the Glutton perusing his family pictures, soured his temperament even more.

Ian's mother, Tracy, made it a project to hang pictures in chronological order. The oldest pictures were hung at the ends of the hallways upstairs and the newest continued through the walls of the stairs into the dining room.

Ronald had a belly that seemed like it was about to pop. He wore a tight buttoned-down white shirt, with suspenders, which he liked to push out using his purlicues. They were meant to hold up his khaki pants, but for some reason he was also wearing an alligator belt. Ian was grateful for one thing, all of the ghosts were fully dressed when they died.

Ronald had noticed Ian without turning and pondered, "How interesting that when you were a baby, you never looked at the camera. But as time passed and you became older, you began to stare at it, fixated, as if trying to force everyone around you out of your sight. I wish you gave me the same attention, like you did, when you were a child."

Ian rolled his eyes. *I'll write about this in my diary later,* he thought. He began walking down the stairs, looking at the pictures of himself that hung on the wall. Each one, a moment frozen in time, his face, serious, full of hatred.

One of the most recent photographs consisted only of the boys: John, his 13-year-old brother, his dad, Benjamin, and himself. Ian's dad held them in front of him in an embrace. He had short black-graying hair, bushy eyebrows, green eyes, a close-trimmed beard and a toothy smile. Ian longed to smile like his father. His eyes moved down the picture, hid dad was dressed in his favorite blue collared shirt.

John and Ian had similar facial features: jet-black hair, straight bushy eyebrows, pointy nose and an angular jawline. The difference was that John wore a side-part hairstyle and had blue-gray eyes, while Ian wore a skater haircut and had loathing gray eyes. Until now, he had never realized how evident it was. The change in his eyes, the dark circles beneath them, the sternness of his face, the tightness of his jaws. He could see the transition through the family pictures from when he started understanding that the majority of his companions were horrible ghosts who were destroying his life. It was as if happiness and joy were literally being sucked from his soul. He smirked. *They won't beat me, plus, being able to notice that sort of change was funny and pleasing...and empowering*, he lied to himself.

Tracy, Ian's mom, had prepared a luscious meal *just* for him. Once a month, she would cook one of the family member's favorite meal. There were five of them; therefore, there were five special days every month, other than birthdays and holidays.

His mother had already served Ian his dish: chicken parmesan buried beneath a mountain of noodles. His chicken was blanketed in thick sticky layers of mozzarella cheese and bathed in red marinara sauce. By time Ian arrived at the table, everyone was quietly munching away.

"Hi, sweetie," cooed his mom. Ian's mom had her brown hair tied up in a loose bun, as she usually did when it came to cooking and eating. She wore bangs, just like Amy, only his mom would blow-dry hers, making it look a little puffier.

Her inviting green eyes and soft face made it seem like she'd never been through any tough times. She wiped her hands on the apron his dad had gifted her on one of their anniversaries. It was light pink with the words

"Incredibly lucky to marry the most beautiful man ever!" embroidered in red across the front. "I've made you a plate. Did you get to finish your homework?" she asked smiling at him.

"Hah! She's trying to pretend like nothing happened while you were upstairs talking to your *imaginary friends*, but they were totally talking behind your back!" laughed Frederick the Scorcher.

Frederick preferred drama from the living, over the yelling and complaining between the other ghosts in Ian's room. They were so uninspiring.

"Yes, mom, thanks for dinner," smiled Ian, ignoring Frederick's taunts.

"No problem, I hope it tastes good, I was running out of the Three Cheese Barilla sauce, so I mixed in some marinara."

"That's fine. Thank you so much," Ian smiled back at her. Frederick continued his tirade, leaning over Ian's shoulder, telling him how upset he should be by his family's horrific behavior.

Ian sat down next to his mom, across from John. His father, Benjamin, sat at the head of the table, next to his mother, and Amy.

Frederick the Scorcher looked like a psychopath. His crazed eyes were the type that made people turn and walk away. Quickly. He had an aquiline nose and pointy ears. Had he not been such a horrible specter, he would have made a terrific elf.

Ian figured he must have either died in prison, or died as a prison escapee, since he was wearing a black-and-white prison uniform.

Frederick pretended to push away from the table and began doing cartwheels around the kitchen. His unkempt, long wavy hair danced around his head, covering his face, all the while he sang, "Backstabbing! Backstabbing!" He came to a stop at the head of the table and pretended to rest his hands on Ian's father's shoulders. "Oh," he oozed, massaging his shoulders, "this is so exciting! I love secrets! How will this turn out? Oh," he jumped up and down, "I can't wait. The excitement's gonna kill me," he said falling backwards, smacking himself in the forehead. "Oh, right, I'm already dead."

Frederick paused and stared directly at Ian with a crazed expression. "Hey, you wanna know what they were saying about you? Well, too bad, I'm not going to tell you. But…if you find out, you're not gonna like it," he laughed in a sing-song voice. "My gut says you wanna know. Oh wait, I don't have one," he moaned making a sad face.

"How's your day been? Anything new?" Tracy asked.

Ian looked at his mom. Obviously, something was up. She had already asked him the same question when he got home from school. Frederick watched the conversation playing out, the anticipation of a galactic breakdown was driving him insane. "Break! Break! Break!" he whispered excitedly in Ian's ear.

"Um," Ian answered, feeling a bit confused, "I already told you…, nothing new."

"Oh," she shook her head, and laughed, "That's right. I must be out of it today."

"Amy was just telling us about your invisible friends?"

Tracy gave John a warning glare, but he pretended not to notice, and continued antagonizing Ian. "You must be really lonely," he smirked. "I mean you gotta create friends just to have friends? How sad is that?"

Unbeknownst to the rest of the family, John used these attacks to somehow try and normalize his brother's behavior. Like it or not, he was caught up in this horrific nightmare that never ended. He'd try to ignore it, but it was all around him. He'd even read books about ghosts and secretly watched horror movies to help conquer his fears, but nothing seemed to help.

Ian usually brushed John's taunts aside, but knowing that they were keeping something from him made this day an exception. "You couldn't be more wrong," he said coldly, "I could never feel lonely because we're never alone." He narrowed his eyes and stared at his brother, "Someone is *always* around."

"Ian, stop trying to scare your brother," said his dad in a gruff manner.

"Why?" Ian asked. Annoyed that his dad defended John, he decided to use Ronald the Glutton's tip from a few nights ago. "Is he still running to your room in the middle of the night?"

"Ian!" Tracy yelled, surprised at his behavior. "Just…stop it!"

"Why should I?" Ian snapped. "He provokes me," pointing at John, "and you *never* do anything."

"That's not true, Ian, and do *not* speak to your mother like that," his dad shouted.

"Treating me unfairly doesn't motivate me to be respectful," Ian retorted.

"Keep going moron," Amy smiled, "you're this close…," she held her pointing finger and thumb five millimeters apart, slowly bringing them together as if squeezing Ian until he was flat, "…to being sent to the shrink."

"Ohhhh, the truth came out! The truth came out!" Frederick laughed gleefully. "What will happen now?! I absolutely positively, demonstratively cannot wait!"

"WHAT?!" Ian stood up, dropping his chair backward. If it weren't for Frederick, he would've thought that Amy was joking.

Tracy glared at Amy, who only shrugged at her. "Calm down Ian, we're not sending you to a shrink," she said looking up at him.

"That's not what you said five minutes ago," Amy explained.

Tracy's jaw dropped. She slammed her hands hard on the table, making the silverware and dishes clink, shocking everyone at the table. "Okay," she breathed, trying to stop herself from yelling. "Amy, you are *so* grounded," she spoke with poison in her voice.

"Grounded?! What's so wrong with being honest?!" Amy protested. "I only repea…."

Ian felt like his head was about to explode. He felt a mixture of anger, sadness and betrayal. "I don't need a shrink!" he interrupted. "I don't have any problems. I'm fine!"

"Ian, sit down," his dad ordered.

"No!" Ian hissed as he stormed off to his bedroom and slammed his door.

"Crazy people don't know they're crazy," Amy tsked.

"Your brother is *not* crazy, Amy," Tracy fussed.

"What?" Amy said, acting innocent. "I just got that from a movie trailer, Hollywood needs to know the influence they have on today's youths."

"As soon as you two are done eating, you're getting ready for bed. I'm done with you," Tracy chided.

"Already?!" Amy cried.

"But it's only 7:30," John argued.

"I don't care!" Tracy's eyes bulged, "I trusted you two." She looked at Ian's untouched food with sad eyes. Her favorite part of the meal was when they would finish the whole plate, but that was taken away from her. She looked at Amy and John, "You two are Ian's siblings and you should be supportive of him. If you continue to deliberately antagonize your brother again, you're all going to get professional help."

John's mouth dropped open, he looked at his mom bewildered, "But m—"

"Period!" Tracy yelled, as they both slumped in their chairs. She grabbed Ian's plate—it was still warm—and headed upstairs. She walked down the left hall to Ian's room and knocked a couple times. "Ian," she said gently.

"Leave me alone," Ian muffled.

"I will leave you alone," Tracy said in her softest voice, "but I don't want you to starve. I'm placing your plate right outside your door. Take your time, but please eat your food. We'll call it a night, okay? Love you." She waited for a response but heard none and sighed. She placed the plate on the floor and walked back downstairs to continue her dinner with the rest of the family.

"Frederiiiick! You down there?!" Xavier yelled out. He melted through Ian's bedroom door searching for him. "What happened? This kid won't tell me nothing. He's all bitter and looks ugly...," his voice trailed off as he reached the dining room.

"You should eat," Helga told Ian.

Ian lay on his bed fuming, his head under his pillow. He was too angry, too hurt, to be hungry. A psychologist.... What a horrible thing to say, hot tears filled his eyes.

"Ian?"

Helga's voice infuriated him all the more. He knew why she wanted him to eat, she needed him to be healthy, because without him, they had no one else from the living to speak to.

Helga hovered over Ian. She considered trying to reason with him, but she decided against it. It wasn't like one night of starving himself would kill him.

Ian pulled his head from below his pillow and turned to look at the clock, it was 7:35 PM. He sighed, *it's not even close to bedtime. Eventually I'll get hungry.... Whatever....*

Ian closed his eyes and decided to try and sleep it off, hoping he'd feel better in the morning. However, Xavier had other plans. He rose up through Ian's floor and started yelling: "*That's* what you're so upset about? Who *cares* if you go to a shrink! Think about how much fun you could have, 'And how do you feel about ghosts?'" he imitated an old lady with a high-pitched voice. "'Well Ms. Shrink, may I call you Martha?'" Xavier toned down his voice, pretending to be Ian, "'I believe that one of the ghosts, he goes by the name, Xavier the Slicer, is the most amazing of them all. He is very interested in you and says he will be watching you tonight while you sleep. Sweet dreams!'" laughed Xavier. "It's an amazing opportunity."

"Don't listen to him, Ian," Peter the Lecher said. "I have more interesting things to say." He was finally getting his moment.

"Dear God, no one cares about you or your girlfriend," groaned Helga, shaking her head. She rolled her eyes as Xavier continued acting out the Day at the Shrink's. "You two are like children. Not belittling children, Ian, you're exceptional."

"You can't belittle anything," Xavier mocked Helga, "you're as big as a battleship."

Peter ignored Helga. He wasn't going to let it go until he shared. "Melody worked out today! She looks, oh so amazing when she sweats. Luckily, she had to take a thorough shower…."

Ian sat up to remove his shoes and socks. He threw his socks one by one at his hamper as if they were basketballs. He scored one and missed the other. *I'll get it in the morning*, he thought. He got up, switched the lights off and dove back in bed.

"Hey! Why'd you turn the lights off? I can't see a thing!" Xavier yelled. "Turn it back on or give us a night light. This is preposterous! Don't tell me you're going to sleep *now*! What are you, five?! Hellooooo!" he wailed.

Ian tried to drown out the sound of the ghosts. He imagined a flock of fluffy sheep. *One, two, three,* he counted loudly in his head, trying to block out the verbal onslaught. The sheep jumped from left to right, one after the other, as if they were jumping lightly on clouds. He reached the thousands and kept counting until he finally drifted off to a fitful sleep, for a few hours.

Chapter 3

He awoke to Xavier's laugh about some ridiculous story he was telling whoever was in the room. Helga kept telling him to shut up and let her meditate. Ian had to pee, but he knew if he got up, they would know he was awake. He opened his left eye, just a fraction and peeked at his clock. *It's only 11:43 PM?!* It was going to be a long night. He let out a groan, got up and stumbled to the hallway in the dark.

"Oh, you're finally awake!" Xavier exclaimed. "Turn on the lights, so Helga can meditate...," he snickered.

Helga and Xavier started fighting again.

Ian opened the door. *Squish.*

"Ugh! What the...," Ian lifted his bare foot. It was covered with cheese, spaghetti sauce and smooshed pasta. Xavier, of course, realized what happened, pointed at Ian and started laughing. "That's karma for keeping us in the dark—or better yet, Parma, like parmesan, get it?" He gripped his sides in a fit of laughter.

Ian pushed the plate out of the way with his smeared foot and hopped single-legged down the hall to the bathroom which was adjacent to his bedroom. He went in and found Felix the Painter waiting for a visitor. "Of course," Ian moaned.

"Ahh," Felix said in an eerily calm soothing voice. "You're the first to come visit me in the middle of the night," he smiled. Felix was hovering by the bathtub. Rays of moonlight shone through the blinds, piercing his body. He had dark brown hair with slivers of gray at the roots. His eyebrows made him look angry even with his big puppy eyes. He wore a black hat with a turned-up brim, and a dark doublet with red sleeves.

Ian flicked on the light, and placed his hand over his eyes, squinting to let them slowly adjust. He washed his foot in the tub before he used the toilet.

"Someone needs to drink more water. You seem a bit dehydrated."

Ian rolled his eyes, washed his hands and flicked out the light.

"I wonder how many more visitors I'll have tonight," mused Felix as Ian walked out the door.

Felix was an odd one and preferred to stay in the bathrooms during the night, letting Ian know who came in and what they did, as if he wanted to know. He already had nightmares about what his brother did alone in his room. He made a mental note to add an observation to his diary: *They never sleep.*

It was 7:00 AM when Ian's alarm went off. He purposely took his time snoozing the alarm, knowing how much it annoyed everyone in his room. They wouldn't let him sleep, so he might as well use any possible way to get on their nerves. Of course, he eventually turned it off before it would start to annoy the living people in the house.

Ian looked at the mirror. He always looked at his eyes to see how bad they looked. All the kids in the school had beautiful white sclera. He'd looked up what that part of the eye was called, because his eyes were always red and swollen—like he had a permanent case of hay fever— and if that wasn't bad enough, his eyes set atop of dark baggy circles. He looked like he'd had a zombie makeover.

Ian stared at his aging face. At this rate, he was going to look thirty before he reached thirteen. *I wonder, if I could actually sleep through the night, if my face would go back to looking like a normal kid. Or,* he wondered, *is this just who I am?*

He studied his hair. Even though it was straight, it was defiant, and unruly. He awoke every morning to find his hair pointing in every direction from all his twisting and turning during the night. He looked like Edward Scissorhands, but with shorter hair.

Xavier was riled up from the alarm clock. "Stop falling in love with yourself and get ready for school, you narcissist! Also, as a special gift, I'm going with you today, for aggravating me with your obnoxious alarm."

Ian shook his head. "Whatever," he whispered. Xavier would've come to the school whether the alarm went off or not….

Suddenly, Ian's heart skipped a beat. He had a history test today. *Dang! I completely forgot!* He felt his anger building. He'd let Frederick and his brother get the best of him, and instead of studying, he'd wasted twelve hours pouting.

He searched through his backpack quickly, took out his binder and flipped through it until he found the history divider. He turned to the last page of his notes. *Okay, the test would consist of World War II. That shouldn't be too hard*, he let out a sigh of relief.

They had seen a short film in class about the war. He couldn't remember much of it because the documentary was constantly interrupted by dead morons attempting to make shadow puppets from the light of the projector. "You're transparent," Ian had hissed, "you can't make shadows," but to no avail.

He closed his eyes, trying to recall anything he could remember from the film. *Oh yeah, the presenter was talking about Adolph Hitler, a vicious dictator and leader of the Nazi party. His insane ideals led him to enforce breeding between blonds and blue eyes to restore the dominant genes of the Nordic-Aryan race. Everyone else was doomed to die. Oddly enough,* Ian recalled, *Hitler had brown hair and blue eyes.* He tapped his finger on his chin, trying to pull fragments of thoughts into a cohesive memory, but nothing useful came to mind, only Helga swooning over the presenter and commenting about his beautiful physique.

Ian continued skimming through his notes, he found that Chapter 8 was going to be on the test.

He grabbed his History textbook out of his bookshelf and searched through the Table of Contents. He found that the chapter was titled *World War II reaches America* and turned to page 53. He flipped through to the end of the section and counted eight pages with hardly any images in them. *Mmm, maybe seven pages without the pictures,* he thought.

He went back to the beginning of the chapter and read through the first page as quickly as possible, looking for dates and any capital letters that popped out at him. Satisfied with his first batch of fresh information, he darted to the bathroom to jump in the shower.

Felix the Painter was standing in the toilet when Ian entered the bathroom. "Do you have a plunger? I seem to have gotten myself stuck," he asked, trying to get Ian's attention.

Ian ignored him. He was busy repeating the history facts he'd just learned in his mind. Luckily, Ian had two things going for him. First, he loved history and he loved his teacher Mr. Griffin. Second, Ian had a remarkable memory, and was fortunate to pass most of his tests with very little studying.

As soon as Ian finished drying himself, he ran through the hallway, careful not to step on the plate…that was no longer there. *Mom must've picked it up*. Everyone else was already downstairs eating. Ian always showered first, followed by John, then Amy. "I'm out!" he yelled, so John could jump in.

He entered his room, shut the door, grabbed his uniform and underwear and brought them to his desk to continue reading while he dressed.

Helga had been watching him running around, "What in the world are you doing, Ian? Do you have a test or something? You seem so agitated."

Xavier inched closer looking at the book. He didn't know how to read and never cared to learn, but he looked at the images and said, "Ohhh, the kid's studying about some war…. This old man looks like Roosevelt. Must be

World War II," he looked up, recalling the past. "That was *such* a joy to watch unfold."

"Ahhh," Helga reminisced. "I only got to live through World War I. It was so much easier to get away with murder. Everyone was so worried about the war...., none of that DNA stuff either."

"Hah! Got to agree with you on that one, fatty. I lived through the American Revolutionary War, and those, by far, were the best years of my life," Xavier smiled.

"I thought you were dead by then," Helga laughed.

"No I wasn't! How many times do I have to say it? I died in 1789! One, Seven, Eight, Nine! Just think of consecutive numbers you stupid oversized pig! STOP LAUGHING!"

Helga convulsed and snorted, causing Xavier to blow up and spew a stream of profanity.

Xavier needed everyone to know everything about him, and he made sure to recount all his living memories to everyone he met. Even if they refused to hear his stories and tried to float away, he would chase them down. So to ask a question about something he had previously mentioned to them was an insult.

Ian, now fully dressed, with a teal shirt, khaki pants and black sneakers, grabbed his book and ran downstairs.

"Good morning, sweetie, did you sleep well?" his mom had already showered and was dressed in a white collared shirt with dark blue dress pants. She wore her wavy brown hair in a wrap-around ponytail and had put on light makeup. She acted as if nothing had happened the night before, which was fine with Ian.

"Mornin'," Ian answered, side stepping her question. He plopped down at the table and scooted a bowl of Honey Nut Cheerios in front of him. He took a big bite of cereal, and then opened his history book to Chapter 8. He read as fast as he could. His history teacher liked to include questions from the entire chapter, and Ian didn't want to be caught off guard. He didn't look up from the book until he heard John come out of the bathroom.

Ian sprang from the table and dashed up the stairs two at a time. He raced down the hall and into the bathroom, so he could brush his teeth before Amy beat him to it.

"Hey!" she yelled, running behind him. "It's my turn! I have school too, you know...."

"Just a minute," he said, already adding toothpaste to his toothbrush.

Amy started counting down while setting up her towel and getting ready, "60...59...58...,"

Ian was done with fifteen seconds to spare and ran out, as Amy slammed the door behind him.

"Boy, you're really in a hurry today, aren't you?" Ronald the Glutton commented.

Ian ran back to his room, slung his backpack over his shoulder, ran downstairs, and grabbed his history book off the table, heading toward the door.

"See you later, Ian…," his dad said in a way that made Ian understand that he wasn't very pleased with his behavior.

Oh well, thought Ian, without stopping, *he's always in a bad mood in the morning.*

"Bye, sweetie, be careful," called out his mom.

Ian waved them goodbye and stepped out of the house into the morning sun. They all walked to school. Ian and John went to the same school, but John preferred to walk on his own. The less time he had to spend or be around his *weirdo* brother, the better.

Ian didn't mind, he enjoyed the few moments of *alone* time. The walk to school was short, Ian had timed himself last year walking a normal pace to school, and it had taken him ten minutes and seventeen seconds to get to school. He figured he should probably time himself again this year because he'd grown four inches, and his stride was probably longer. He'd try to remember to do that today after school. Ian opened his textbook, found where he had left off and began reading again, only looking up when he had to cross the street.

"Ow, watch it kid," snapped an old man.

Ian was so into his history book that he didn't even notice he'd stepped on the old man's foot. He kept walking without breaking stride.

"Kids these days," the old man grumbled.

Xavier followed closely behind him along with a few of his *friends*. "Look at him, he's not paying attention to anything," Xavier explained to them, "I think he has a test today."

"Ohhh," his friends answered.

"What made you decide to go to school today?" Lucas the Teaser asked Xavier. Lucas had very short dark hair, a long head, small eyes, a bumpy nose and big lips. He wore blue overalls over his shirt, reminding Ian of a miner.

"The kid likes to push my buttons, so I'm gonna push his. He thinks he can get away with being a pompous little brat, so...I need to put him in his place," he explained puffing up his chest.

"That's great!" Lucas exclaimed. "How are you going to do that?"

"My very presence disturbs him, so just being around should do the trick," he smiled. "But if I need to be...shall we say, a little more aggressive, I can do that too." The other ghosts laughed nervously.

Ian was half-listening to Xavier's incessant blabbering. He was used to him boasting to his friends about how terrifying he was. Ian turned a page in his history book and slammed into a tall woman carrying a tray full of coffee.

"Hey, watch where you're going!" she yelled angrily.

"Sorry, I thought you were dead," Ian muttered without looking up.

The lady gasped and ran to the nearest window to look at herself in the reflection.

"I love it!" Xavier yelled. "He's going to mow down every person on the sidewalk. This is better than shark week."

Ian was used to bumping into people, especially when he wasn't paying attention, which was more often than not. There were so many dead people mixed in with the living that mistakes were bound to happen. On the average day, when going to school, Ian would walk through fifteen to twenty dead people. Occasionally, he wouldn't react fast enough, and he'd collide with a living person.

At first, Ian was extremely apologetic. "I'm so sorry, I'm so clumsy," and "I'm sorry I was distracted," but after years of this happening, he'd become jaded, his favorite response had become: "Sorry, I thought you were dead." Ian thought it elegantly conveyed everything that needed to be said. There was an apology, and then a reason, who could expect more from a twelve-year-old boy?

Ian bumped into six more people until he finally reached his school. He glanced at his watch, it was almost 8:00 AM. School didn't start until 8:30 AM, which was perfect because it gave him another thirty minutes to cram for his test.

The halls were mostly empty. Ian snuck past the front desk avoiding being sent to before-care: where students had to go so they could be supervised by adults, until school started. Ian hid in the doorway of the art room as two teachers passed by heading toward the teacher's lounge. He checked the hallway once again, and then dashed to the classroom. He let out a sigh of relief, the door was unlocked.

Xavier and his friends followed Ian into his classroom, a group of ghosts were already there. "Boo!" yelled a skinny ghost that resembled a hotdog. "That never gets old," he laughed, high-fiving another ghost dressed like a cashier.

The ghosts huddled around Xavier as he updated them on what had occurred since he last saw them. A nerdy looking ghost with a comb-over and super thick glasses revealed what he had learned while hanging out in the teacher's lounge.

Ian rolled his eyes and dropped his backpack next to his desk and slid into his chair. *Alright,* he flipped through Chapter 8, *only two pages left.* He glanced at the clock. He just about had thirty minutes before school started. That was plenty of time to finish the chapter, and then skim through it again. The actual test wasn't until 10:30 AM, but once school started, he wouldn't get a chance to study any more.

Ian ignored the steady flow of students trickling into the classroom. It wasn't until a tangible hand waved between his eyes and his book, that he finally looked up. To his great disappointment, it was Madison Greyhart.

Chapter 4

"Good morning!" she yelled cheerfully at Ian. Her endless happiness and energy drove him insane. "So odd to see you studying at school. You didn't get to study at home?"

"No," Ian answered and went back to reading.

"You'll do fine!" Madison yelled. She was always yelling. Ian figured she had been a football coach in a previous life, if there was one. Even Xavier turned his head to see who was interrupting him.

Madison leaned back in her chair, her long brown hair flowed down her shoulders, onto his desk and finally settling over his book. She twisted her head to the side, looking over her shoulder at Ian. "The teacher is here!" she sang.

Ian groaned in annoyance. He leaned back in his chair, trying to create as much space as possible between him, and her annoying smile.

She gazed at him, her hazel eyes twinkling in the morning sunlight. She could care less if Ian found her bothersome. Someday, she'd win him over.

Ian shut his history textbook, threw it in his backpack, and pulled out his geography and social studies books. This was going to be a long day.

If only everyone could see what I see, thought Ian. Several ghosts *sat* on the edge of students' desks, listening to the teacher, absorbing the material. Ian guessed that many of them had never had the opportunity to attend a real school and found the lecture fascinating. They breathed oohs and aahs as they were enlightened.

Other ghosts would go around the class to see what students were doodling, or writing on their notebook or scraps of paper, meant for another classmate. The invisible snoops would yell out to each other.

"Kara's a pretty good artist."

"Mark is hiding a comic book in his geography book."

"Ooh," called out one of the ghosts, "Spiderman, I love Spiderman." He floated in the air pretending to shoot a web at one of his friends.

Xavier was cackling away about who had a crush on who, making nasty remarks about the students in love.

Ian always tried taking notes in class, but it was incredibly difficult with all of the distractions. He did his best to copy what his teacher wrote on the board, but he'd usually end up with one or two sentences in his notebook. Meanwhile, while he struggled, Madison wrote page after page of notes.

Madison always made it a goal to write every single word the professors said.

She'd make a great court stenographer, thought Ian. *Aren't those the people that have to write really quickly?* He wasn't really sure, and he really didn't care.

Every day, every class ends the same, thought Ian. Madison would turn to Ian and tell him to have a super swell day, and then she'd rush to, Mrs. Wiles, the librarian, and pay her to photocopy all of her notes. Then she'd track down Ian, give him her notes, and then bombard him with a zillion questions about ghosts. She felt that information for notes was definitely a fair exchange.

Most of the time Ian would refuse her notes; she couldn't figure out if it was from embarrassment or pride or maybe he felt guilty, because most of her questions about ghosts went unanswered. Whatever it was, she was determined to earn his friendship and gain his trust. So, when he refused her notes, she would wait for the right moment, and surreptitiously jam them in his backpack.

In the end, he needed them, he just never wanted to admit it. Admitting it would mean that Madison was actually helpful...and that was too much of a burden to bear.

"Ian! Are you listening to me?" yelled Mrs. Fernandez.

Ian's head snapped up at her, returning to reality. *Dang! I didn't hear her.* "What?!" he shouted back.

He could barely make out what she was asking him with all the ghostly noise in the room. "What?" he asked again. "I'm sorry, I'm having a hard time hearing you."

That was the last straw for Mrs. Fernandez. "Ian," she pointed a trembling finger at him, "go stand in the corner for the rest of the class."

Ian let out an exasperated sigh. He didn't need to hear her to know what she wanted him to do. He slid out of the desk and went to go stand in the corner. Oddly, the sound of his classmates laughing at him came through loud and clear. He felt something mushy and wet hit him in the back of the neck, a spitball. He felt the tips of his ears grow bright red; this made his classmates laugh even harder.

Even though Ian was in the sixth grade, Mrs. Fernandez seemed to enjoy treating the students like they were first graders. Ian was sure she enjoyed humiliating and embarrassing him in front of his classmates.

Ian let out a sigh of relief when the class finally ended. He rushed over to his desk. He didn't want Mr.

Griffin, his favorite teacher, seeing him standing in the corner.

Madison turned in her seat to face Ian. She felt badly for him. "Have you gone to an audiologist?" she asked softly. Ian didn't answer, and then she realized he might not be able to hear a word she was saying. "Have you been to an audiologist?!" she asked much louder.

"What are you babbling about?" Ian snapped. "I'm trying to study."

"An audiologist. It's a person that can test your hearing."

"I can hear just fine," Ian replied harshly. "Now let me study."

"Good morning everyone," Mr. Griffin boomed enthusiastically. Xavier jumped in front of the gangly teacher, gyrating his hips, salsa dancing across the front of the room. "I hope you're ready for your test!" His eyes sparkled when he said the last word. "If everyone finishes the test ten minutes before the class ends, I'll take you to the cafeteria and buy you a snack."

From the way the class cheered, you would think they hadn't eaten in a month. Ian knew the real reason Mr. Griffin was so excited about going to the cafeteria. It was Mrs. Nelson. She was the new dessert chef, and Mr. Griffin was madly in love with her. Ian hadn't figured this out on his own—it was only because he was privy to the

Smedlys, a group of ghosts that prided themselves on knowing all of the gossip going on in the school.

So, like clockwork, even if the students hadn't finished their test, they would race to Mr. Griffin's desk, and turn their paper in...just for an ice cream sandwich or pudding pop.

Mr. Griffin grabbed the test papers off his desk and then counted the number of students in each row. The student at the front would take a stack from him, take a test, and then pass it to the person behind them and so on. Madison passed Ian a stack and gave him a sugary smile.

He grabbed one and passed the others behind him without turning his head. As soon as they grabbed the tests from him, he started writing his name and date at the top and began reading his test.

1.   When did World War II begin and end? Give exact dates.

2.   What event caused World War II to start?

3.   Which were the first countries to declare war?

4.   Where did the French's surrender to Germany take place?...

Twenty-five questions...and forty minutes...so almost two minutes a question, I got this. Ian began answering them as fast as possible. He skimmed through the test, answering the ones that he knew, deciding to come back and attack the ones that he wasn't so sure of later. He'd made it through fifteen questions when Xavier and his cohorts dispersed throughout the classroom, shouting to each other.

The ghosts' shouts and laughter grew louder and louder, Ian pressed his palms against his ears trying to concentrate. "Oh my God, you should see what this kid wrote," one of them screamed. His voice tore through Ian's brain like fingernails across a chalkboard.

"Isn't that sweet of her? She must like Ian," said one of Xavier's friends. Ian looked up to see what he was talking about. Madison had been picking up the top of her paper slightly so Ian could copy off of her. Ian refused to cheat and went back to working on his test.

"Hah! Xavier, this kid right here thinks Hitler made the French surrender on a boat! He has quite the imagination," laughed Lucas the Teaser.

"Oh, it was on a train car! Hitler used the train car Germany surrendered in during World War I to humiliate France in World War II. Even *I* know that!" Xavier laughed, and got excited for knowing the answer to a question. "Keep reading more questions, I bet I can answer all of them. That was my favorite time period!"

"Oh, let's play trivia!" suggested another ghost.

They all gathered around Lucas as he began reading questions from the test. The other ghosts shouted out answers as fast as they could. Ian dropped his head onto his hands and started ruffling his hair in frustration. He tried to block out their voices, but it was impossible—with everyone else so quiet, the ghosts were all he could hear. *How am I supposed to know if I would've figured out the answers on my own?*

"Where were most of the concentration camps located?" Lucas asked.

"Poland!" most yelled.

"Germany!" yelled Mary the Sloth.

"No, stupid! It was Poland!" Xavier spat. "How can you get that one wrong? These questions are ridiculously easy! You suck!"

"Don't call me stupid, you old disgusting b…."

Mary and Xavier began fighting, until Lucas calmly said, "Why are you complaining, Xavier? She doesn't get a point, and you do…."

While Xavier and his cronies were arguing over who got what point for what answer, Ian was struggling with a moral dilemma. He hadn't even read through all of the questions, and there they were, shouting out the answers. He couldn't help but hear them. *Is it cheating if I remember reading about what they're discussing?*

Ian started tapping his pencil's eraser on his desk. What was the right thing to do? It wasn't like he could ask anyone, only himself. He looked down at his test. He couldn't help but know the answers to them now. Hesitantly, he filled in the blanks. He was just about to finish the last question when he heard a voice.

"Cheating, are we Ian?"

He jumped so harshly, he banged his knee under his desk, hitting the metal frame. He immediately held his knee and tried to stifle a whimper. He looked back, to see if it was Mr. Griffin.

"Ian! What are you doing? Keep your eyes on your test! If I catch you cheating, you're going straight to the principal's office!" barked Mr. Griffin, who had been sitting at his desk, staring daggers at him. Ian cursed under his breath, it wasn't his teacher; it was one of Xavier's friends who had startled him.

All the ghosts began oohing and laughing. "Detention! Detention! Detention!" shouted Lucas the Teaser, marching around the room like a soldier.

Ian, frustrated, finished the test by stabbing the paper with his pencil as if he were trying to hurt it. He stood and limped to Mr. Griffin, with hatred in his eyes, slammed his test on the teacher's desk, and walked out. He could hear the chorus of ghosts chanting, "Cheater…cheater…cheater."

Outside, there was a rectangular garden, surrounded by waist-high concrete walls. A series of benches were placed around a rock garden. There used to be flowering bushes and plants, but students complained that they gave them allergies, and attracted bees—so now, they had a concrete wall, surrounding a garden of rocks....

Still, the garden was a favorite place for students to gather after lunch to catch up with their friends until it was time for their next class. Ian looked up from his bench, just in time to see Mr. Griffin walk by, followed by a row of students. Ian thought they looked ridiculous, all waddling along behind him, on the way to the cafeteria.

Ian wondered what grade he'd get on his test. He was sure Mr. Griffin would give him a low score now. It didn't help that a few of the ghosts had followed him outside—they were teasing him and taunting him, telling him that cheating was only the beginning. "Soon, you'll be just like us," they laughed.

Ian closed his eyes. *Is there a point to me being here?* he thought, while caressing his knee. *I do learn some, I guess, but I'm constantly punished. Punished because of others...others that can't be seen. If I were homeschooled, I wouldn't have this problem. I wouldn't have teachers that think I'm an idiot, who think that I just act out because I'm a problem child. I'm not.*

"Hey!"

Nooooo, Ian facepalmed. *She's heeeere....*

"You finished the test really fast," Madison smiled, sitting next to him. "I hope you aced it. It was kind of easy, wasn't it?"

Ian shrugged.

Madison stared at him. She pursed her lips, deep in thought as to what to say next. "That was the first time you've ever turned in your test before time was up. Did you get help?" she asked hesitantly, and then quickly threw her hands up, "I promise I won't tell anybody." She knew he didn't copy off of her since he finished his test before her.

Ian felt embarrassed and angry, he answered her question without answering it. "I thought you watched me studying."

Madison stopped herself from making him feel more uncomfortable, so she smiled instead, "Oh yeah, that's right. I'm sure you did well. Great job!" She patted him on the back, making Ian glare at her. "So...how is everyone doing? Are there many around today?" she asked, looking up at the sky, avoiding Ian's expression.

Here she goes again....

"Were there some in the classroom? Are they smart? I bet they're good at history...." Madison went on and on, so Ian muted her out, and finally walked away, to a place she couldn't follow him, the boy's bathroom.

Chapter 5

Ian bolted out of the school and into the sunlight. It was Friday and he was looking forward to the weekend. He took his time walking home, making sure he didn't bump into anyone. He wanted to make it through the weekend without anyone yelling at him.

He waited for a car to pass at Evergreen Avenue, and then crossed over onto This Way Street. He always thought the name of his street was quite peculiar. He imagined it caused a lot of confusion. If he had any friends, he could test out the theory…maybe someday.

Ian's house was in the middle of the block. It was the only white house with brown shutters. Every other house had a tint of blue or green with colorful shutters. Ian's house simply looked boring. He shuffled up the sidewalk, his knee still ached a little—he really smacked it good. He pushed open the door, and saw that John was already home and speaking to his mother.

"Hi sweetie, how was your day?" she smiled with sad eyes, still affected by what happened the night before.

"It was fine, thanks," he replied and headed toward his room.

"Ian," his mom stopped him, "John had an idea…that you may like. Why don't you hear him out?"

John stared at her, wondering why she put him on the spot. Obviously, he wanted *her* to tell him about it.

Ian rested his back on the banister and stared at John, waiting.

"Um," John started nervously. "I know you're having a tough time with your ghosts…."

Ian raised an eyebrow.

"I'm not making fun, okay? But, I heard that priests can exorcise or bless houses and it can get rid of them," John continued, "Then you don't have to deal with ghosts anymore."

Heard? Ian thought. *Obviously, he watched another rated R movie last night. Probably "The Exorcist."*

"Would you like that honey? We could do it this weekend. Only if you're comfortable with that of course," his mom said.

"Go for it." He paused. He knew John was doing this just as much for himself as he was for him, but John had reached out. "And thank you John," Ian said weakly.

John's mouth dropped open. Had Ian actually thanked him? He watched as Ian turned and walked up the stairs.

"You're not going to get rid of us that easily, I hope you know," Xavier smiled. He had been following behind him. He told Helga, Frederick, Peter and Felix about the exorcism to get them all excited for the weekend.

Everything was pretty much back to normal with his family. They didn't bring up the shrink and his parents arranged for a priest to come over on Sunday to bless the house. The ghosts were celebrating and anxious for the priest to arrive.

Sunday, 2:03 PM.

Ian was just finishing a clementine in the kitchen when he heard a knock on the door. His dad ran out of the kitchen to open it. "I think it's the priest," he exclaimed excitedly.

Frederick and Felix came to have a look.

His dad looked through the peephole, and then opened the door.

Ian walked toward the door, curious to see who it was. The man looked to be in his 40s. He was about 5 foot 7, a little round in the belly; he wore a black cassock, had a cross in his left hand, and a bottle of what was presumed to be holy water in his right hand.

"Thank you so much for coming," his dad said to the priest. "Please come in."

"Oh yes, thank you." The priest entered and used his sleeve to wipe some of the sweat from his forehead.

"Look at him. He's so nervous, is he even trained for this?" Frederick the Scorcher was laughing.

Felix the Painter answered, "He seems to be disoriented. It's probably his first time. This is going to be great!"

"Oh, you're here!" Ian's mother exclaimed, rushing into the living room. "Thank you so much for coming!"

"It's my pleasure," he smiled weakly, looking around.

"This is my son, Ian," Ben held Ian by the shoulder. "He's the one who can…sort of sense spirits I guess you could say."

"Oh I see. Hi Ian, nice to meet you," he held his hand out awkwardly to Ian, but then at the last second he pulled it away.

"He probably thinks that spirits are contagious," snickered Felix the Painter. "I hope he's got plenty of Purrell."

"In what area do you experience the most supernatural activity?"

"In my pants!" yelled Peter the Lecher, who had surprisingly heard the priest from Ian's room.

"Over here!" Xavier yelled from Ian's room. "Yoo-hoo!"

Ian could hear Helga laughing.

"Emit some ghostly power," Ian could hear Xavier telling the others, "maybe he can *sense* our presence if we try and force some of our spirit to spread."

"You look like you're about to explode from constipation," Helga snorted.

"I'm trying to show him the way, you moron! Stop being a lazy hippo and emit some ghostly essence!" Xavier snapped at her.

"Ian, would you like to show…um," Tracy turned to the priest.

"Father Robert," he answered her.

"Thank you. Please show Father Robert to your room."

Ian nodded and pointed up, "Upstairs."

"At least we're going up," joked Father Robert uncomfortably. "You know," he clarified seeing the confused looks on Ian's parents' faces, "closer to heaven."

Father Robert followed Ian up the stairs, Ian's parents behind the priest. His brother and sister were in their rooms, watching TV, as if this were an everyday occurrence…most likely, they were scared to death of the exorcism.

"We don't really hear or see anything out of the ordinary," his mother explained to Father Robert, "but Ian seems to be more…should I say, sensitive to the dead."

"I see," Father Robert nodded. "How interesting."

Ian opened his door and stood by his bed, letting the priest come in. His parents stood by the doorway.

Xavier was celebrating…. Helga and Peter were watching curiously.

The other ghosts gathered outside the room to watch the show as well.

With trembling hands, Father Robert opened the bottle of holy water and thrust the massive bronze cross out in front of him.

"In the name of Jesus, bring peace and rid of the evil spirits dwelling in this room," Father Robert demanded. He shook the bottle of holy water, sprinkling it toward the left side of Ian's room.

"The evil spirits are over there," Ian pointed toward the right, past his bed, where Xavier was mooning him.

"I'm about to emit some spiritual essence," Xavier roared.

Father Robert just uttered, "Oh." He sprinkled holy water at Xavier's feet and repeated his prayer.

Xavier's eyes bulged. He began shaking uncontrollably. "What's happening?" he looked down at his body. "I'm…I'm melting!" he yelled, "I'm melting!" He placed his hand over his heart and reached his left hand toward the sky.

Ian began to smile, watching as Xavier slowly started to disappear through the floor.

Helga burst out laughing at Xavier's stupidity, making Ian's face fall. He understood her laugh. He realized Xavier was just pretending to disappear by going through the floor, only to end up on the first floor. Xavier then yelled, "Alright, I'm coming back upstairs!"

"This room is now blessed," Father Robert stated. "I will bless the other rooms just to make sure the evil spirits are truly gone."

Ian wanted to vomit.…

Chapter 6

During dinnertime, his parents asked Ian if the blessing of the house helped at all.

If I say yes, they won't bother me about it anymore, if I say no, the next step may be a shrink. "I hope so," is all he could think to say. He didn't want to lie, but he wanted his parents to stop talking and worrying about it. It was his problem, and his problem alone. There was nothing they could do about it. Luckily, they were happy with Ian's answer and changed the subject.

After dinner, Ian went to his room, opened his diary and put on his headphones. He just needed a moment of silence. He couldn't imagine what life must be like to not be accosted by ghosts, night and day…every day of his life.

He knew his brother had been hopeful, that his whole family had been hopeful that the priest would be able to help, but Ian knew in his heart, the moment he saw Father Robert, that he was no match for Xavier and his friends. Now the ghosts became even more unbearable, realizing that the exorcism held no power over them.

"I guess we're not evil spirits," Peter commented.

"Pffffft, yeah right," Xavier replied.

"It probably only works with demons. Maybe we just can't see the demons and he got rid of them. I do feel a little lighter," Helga mused.

"Aha…. That'll never happen. Accept that you'll always be rotund," Xavier swooped his arms around in front of him as if he had a giant belly.

Ian's pencil scratched against the paper, his first sentence: Exorcism does not work!

Ian explained how the day went, from the moment the priest came until he left. Then he decided to write about each of the ghosts. Maybe writing it down in his diary will make him feel better about life and he could accept his fate. Just to spite Xavier, he began to write about Sneaky Helga first.

Ian smiled; he knew how angry Xavier would be if he found out that he wasn't the first ghost in his diary.

Sneaky Helga

- *Probably weighed about a ton when she was alive. Now she's lighter than a feather because she's a ghost. She wears a short red dress with pearls as accessories. She has dark red hair slicked back and a lot of prominent facial features. The most striking feature was her lips. They matched her huge body.*

- *Her voice sounds extremely rough, as if she had smoked her entire life.*

- *When she was alive, she was the queen of an underground organization of women. They called her Madam in her establishment. After she advanced her career from being a 'lady of the night', she no longer felt she needed to keep her petite figure and destroyed it with endless brownies and bunt cake. Had she lived in Hershey, Pennsylvania, she would have probably eaten the city.*

- *She was later named Sneaky Helga because she would kill her victims without them ever noticing she was around. Her victims were usually the ones who didn't pay for their services or harmed her employees. She was murdered in the 1920s out of vengeance for a family member she targeted.*

- *She hardly ever leaves my room. It's extremely rare when she does, but she's usually around me. She's always attempting to meditate, but the others like to interrupt her.*

Peter the Lecher

- *He looks like Mr. Monopoly but with dark hair. He even wears similar clothes. His striking feature: a dark bushy mustache that looks like a hairy bowtie pointing upward and waxed at the tips.*

- *He was probably into opera, not only because of what he's wearing, but also because he always likes to speak with a sort of poetic rhythm. Everything he says is spoken with a dramatic flair.*

- *When he was alive, he searched for women that he wanted to spend the rest of his life with. But none of them met his expectations and so he would get rid of them. He died from a vicious knife attack. He never said when he died, but if I have to guess, from the style of his clothes, it may have been in the mid-1900s. After he died, he ventured around and finally found the woman of his dreams, a living person, her name is Melody. How ironic.*

- *Peter comes over every night to tell me about Melody. He loves talking about her, but…she would not like to hear what he has to say.*

Frederick the Scorcher

- *He looks like he just came out of an asylum because he won't ever stop moving and twisting his head left and right like a bird. It's surprising that he's not wearing a straitjacket. Instead, he's wearing clothes from prison. Black and white stripes like an umpire, only horizontal. Striking features: untidy long hair and big searching eyes.*

- *He talks a mile a minute. He likes to ask himself questions and then answer them. He prefers to watch the living people and gets really excited if anything horrible is happening.*

- *I'm not sure who he targeted. It seems like his victims were random, but he liked to burn them.*

- *I'm not sure how he died, but I'm guessing he was probably murdered. He probably drove someone nuts.*

- *He generally stays in the kitchen. He's still very excited about being able to float around and do tricks in the air.*

Felix the Painter

- *He always looks angry, even when he's calm. Striking feature: angry eyebrows. He wears simple clothes; I'm guessing because he loves to paint.*

- *He talks in a calm eerie manner. He's weird and creepy.*

- *When he was alive, he would spy on people. He painted them on a canvas, then he would kill them. He said that his victims lived in his canvas and they were no longer needed in the world. The memory of them was already in his paintings. Once killed, he would then paint their faces black, as if erasing them.*

- He said that one day he just never woke up. He doesn't know how he died.

- He haunts the bathroom and hates glade plug-ins.

Ronald the Glutton

- Helga looks more like a gelatinous blob. Ronald has more of a round hard belly. He wears suspenders, like my grandpa. I'm guessing he probably died in the 1900s.

- Ronald is more of an observer. Sometimes I don't even notice he's around until he talks to me.

- He was a cannibal when he lived. I'm not going into details about it.

- I don't know if he died naturally or if he was killed, and I don't care to ask.

- He likes to venture around. He doesn't bother me as much as the others, but he tends to complain about not getting enough attention.

Mary the Sloth

- *She is tall, has puffy brown hair and a face like Marilyn Monroe's. She wears a life vest over an evening gown. She has long white gloves, a scarf around her neck, and is barefoot.*
- *She was actually a passenger on the Titanic. She was escaping Southampton, New England, to get away with murder. She wasn't a first-class lady...she just stole clothes from the rich and wore them so no one would think twice about her identity.*
- *She didn't kill anyone on the Titanic, she just stole from them. She tends to be very lazy, so she hated high-energy people. She would end up killing them in a slow manner...lazily.*
- *She's not very bright, but she thinks very highly of herself because of her looks and because she died in the 'unsinkable' ship. She has rare bursts of energy if something exciting is happening, otherwise she is slow and sluggish.*
- *She sank with the Titanic, so she died in 1912. Karma did her in.*

Xavier the Slicer

- *He looks insane, similar to Frederick the Scorcher. His eyes are oddly large. He wears* military clothes, which were completely out-of-date during his time.

- *He's* extremely *annoying. Probably the most annoying of them all. He loves attention. He's loud* all *the time. His main goal is to find his killer so he can avenge his death. Unfortunately for him, he doesn't have the slightest clue of who killed him, this makes me believe that they don't become ghosts immediately after they die. If they did, Xavier would've probably seen the culprit trying to hide his lifeless body—which was gone when he appeared at his place of death.*

- *Xavier would wear the military clothes from his late father when he hunted for people. He loved to pretend like he was a ghost from the past that came to haunt his prey and kill them with his sword. He loved how theatrical it felt.*

- *He can also be very stupid, like Mary the Sloth, but he'd never admit it. He belittles everyone else to feel good about himself.*

- *He died in 1789, from a gunshot to the heart.*

- *He haunts my bedroom night and day.*

Lucas the Teaser

- *Lucas looks and acts normal. He's attractive (for a ghost) and dresses well, with a suit and tie.*

- *Lucas hid his insanity extremely well. It was hard to believe that he was a murderer.*
- *Lucas charmed women and kidnapped them. Then he teased them into believing that he would not hurt them and will let them go free. In the end, before they lost all hope of freedom, he killed them. He loved to play with people's emotions.*
- *He died in the 1980s. Someone poisoned him at a convention. Unlike Xavier, he doesn't care to learn who killed him, he loves the fact that it's a mystery.*
- *He mostly haunts the streets and likes to watch people.*

~~Madison the Master Annoyer~~
- *~~She looks innocent, but when she opens her mouth, it feels like my world is ending….~~*
- *~~She…She….~~*

I'll come back to her later, Ian decided.

Ian sat back in his chair, satisfied with his plan to make Xavier seem less important. He had purposely put Xavier's description in the middle of his diary entry. That way—if he ever finds out about it—Xavier wouldn't think he was the last one to linger on Ian's mind, or suggest that Ian simply left the best for last.

He felt a sense of accomplishment. It had taken him a couple of hours to write about each of them. It felt good to have some order amidst the uncontrollable chaos in his life. He didn't mention every ghost he knew since some weren't in his life as much.

Ian held his pencil by the middle, between his fingers and tapped the eraser end on his desk. *The ones I mentioned and the ones I left out, all murdered at least one person. Interesting. I can't believe I never thought about it before….*

Ian removed his headphones and stretched his arms. "Hmm," he thought out loud, enough for those only in his room to hear, "I wonder if every single dead wanderer was a murderer…." He could see that he'd caught their attention through his peripheral vision. "What could have happened to all the other sinners?" He put the tip of the eraser at the end of his lip, deep in thought.

They're so quiet now…. Do they even know?

"What do you think, Helga?" Ian asked quietly, still watching them through the corner of his eye.

"That's a first," she replied. "I never would've thought you'd ask me anything again. But I don't know and never really cared to think it through."

Peter the Lecher said, "Same here, I prefer living my life up to the fullest while I'm still here."

Life? Ian raised his eyebrow.

"Why constantly worry about the past? Life's too short, I don't have the time to waste thinking about what could have been," Peter explained. "Speaking of time," he looked at Ian's alarm clock, "Melody should be back home for her shower. Gotta go!" He passed through the wall, gone from sight.

Xavier miraculously hadn't answered yet. Ian could see him with his arms crossed, tapping his right pointing finger on his left arm...waiting for Ian's attention, but refusing to cooperate.

Ian sighed, "Well I guess everyone is downright clueless...."

"You didn't ask me!" Xavier shouted. "Don't group me in with the stupids!"

"Oh," Ian smiled internally. "So you actually know?"

"Hah! Wouldn't *you* like to know?"

Ian stared right at Xavier. Xavier felt strangely uncomfortable. *What is this crazy feeling?* It was close to panic, and he didn't like panic. Xavier remained quiet, refusing to talk.

Ian's eyes narrowed. "You know nothing," he scoffed.

He could see that Xavier was about to explode from the insult, but then calmed himself. "Fine, young Ian, I'll tell you...but what's in it for me?"

"Okay," Ian pretended to ponder. "I may consider finding your killer."

Xavier's interest instantly peaked. It's as if he vomited the words out, "I believe it's a lot like *Dante's Inferno*. There are different stages of Hell. Obviously, we're at one of the first stages. Most people believe that murderers go straight to the fiery pit of Hell where we'll be tortured for all of eternity...but look at us," he gestured with his arms showing the room, "we're living the dream. Helga gets to stay fat forever, Peter gets to watch Melody until she dies, I get to have the chance of finding my killer. I'd say it's those who aren't full-fledged sinners that are being tortured. I bet the Devil is punishing them for not being evil enough. We're like the cream of the crop. It's as if he puts us up on the highest pedestal for bringing his sickest dreams to reality."

Ian had heard of *Dante's Inferno*, but he'd never thought about reading the story, besides, it was fiction. Furthermore, Ian had seen things that would make Dante's head spin. But then again, Ian stared at the floor, deep in thought—*maybe Xavier was correct to some extent...could it be that murderers are the least punished? That can't be true.* He looked Xavier in the eyes. "So you're saying that all of you will stay around for good, until I die?"

Xavier thought about that for a moment, he wasn't enjoying this conversation.

"Actually," Helga added. "It's not forever. Eventually we will disappear."

Xavier scowled at Helga, obviously keeping that piece of information to himself.

"Disappear?" Ian whispered.

"Yes," Xavier spat, "but that won't happen for a *very* long time."

"How long?" Ian's eyes sparkled.

"Mmm, sorry to break it to you kiddo," Helga said, "but it's several hundreds of years after we die. You see, time stops for us, so I guess for the deities, if there are any, they go by their own clocks. A millennium for the living is probably only an hour for them. But I've seen a couple of us disappear, and I know they died in the early 1000s...."

"Anyways!" Xavier interrupted, annoyed that Helga had revealed so much. "Now that we told you what you want to know, when will you keep your part of the bargain and find my killer?"

Ian went back to writing and then responded calmly, "I said I *may* consider finding your killer."

Xavier's head was at the brink of exploding. "You disgusting little son of a…!" profanity flew from his mouth. He rushed at Ian threw his hands around his neck and squeezed with all his might. "I wish I could just…choke you to death!" he growled.

"Keep trying," Ian continued writing, unperturbed.

Xavier screamed in frustration, as if it would somehow give him the power to hurt him.

"Oh no," Ian mocked, "I must be dying now."

Chapter 7

Ian woke up to a stormy Monday morning. Outside, the trees were swaying back and forth. He could hear the *tap, tap, tap* of the branches, clicking like skeletal fingers on his window. He turned and looked at his clock. *Darn*, he moaned. It was 6:59 AM, only one minute before his alarm went off.

Beep, beep!

Ian slammed the snooze button and saw everyone turn to him.

Xavier wasn't there, which surprised Ian. *He must be still fuming about last night.... Good.*

He sat up in bed, for the first time, in a long time, Ian felt like he had actually slept through the night. *Must have been the noise from the storm*, he thought.

Ian hurriedly got dressed and raced down for breakfast. He was tired yet anxious to know what grade he received for his history test. Ian scarfed down a bowl full of Cheerios, shoved his chair back under the table, and grabbed his backpack and hoodie.

Ian was about to step out the door, when his mom stopped him. "Hold it!" she yelled. "You're not walking to school in this weather. I'm dropping you off today."

"I need to get there early."

"For what?" she snapped, obviously in a bad mood.

"Nothing," he groaned. "Just wanted to see what I got on my history test."

"Oh," his mom hesitated for a moment. "We'll be ready in five minutes."

As fate would have it, the storm worsened as he waited for his mother and John to get ready. The trio had to sprint to the minivan to avoid getting soaked. Ian had to admit, his mom was right, it was absolutely pouring outside. He'd be soaked if he'd walked. Despite the heavy traffic, she got them to school on time.

John slid the car door open, revealing Hell on Earth. "We should have taken the boat this morning, mom."

Ian groaned loudly without thinking about who was listening.

"Just run for it," encouraged Tracy, "a little rain won't hurt you."

John dashed out as he yelled, "Bye mom!"

"Bye John! Bye Ian!"

"Bye!" Ian yelled back, and ran right through Xavier, who had been standing there waiting for him, a strange twisted smile on his face. "Well good morning, you worthless twerp! Did you think you would get rid of me that easily?" His friends floated behind him, ready to enjoy their day at school.

Ian ran through the doors and slipped on a small puddle on the beige-tiled floor. He watched as his legs flew up into the air, he braced himself for the impact which thankfully was cushioned by his backpack.

Xavier and his friends surrounded him, roaring with laughter.

"Oh you poor baby!" Xavier yelled, with his hands on his knees, leaning forward toward him. He extended his hand. "Here, let me help you up. Whoops! No can do!" he took his hand back and laughed hysterically.

Ian sat up and shook his head. Xavier and his friends circled around Ian, mocking him. Normally, the other ghosts wouldn't have come along to accompany him to school, but Xavier must've asked for extra help today.

Ian was so immersed in their mockery, he didn't realize that other students had watched him fall and were laughing too.

Ian stared at the students and gave them a smile. He took out one of his notebooks and a pen. He looked at one student and scribbled on his notebook, stared at another student and wrote again. He continued staring at them and writing calmly, until they started realizing that he was writing their names down in his notebook.

"He's going to curse us!" someone yelled. They all started screaming and ran and slid everywhere, trying to get out of Ian's sight.

"Hmmm…clever," Lucas nodded in admiration.

"Shut up Lucas!" Xavier screamed. "Don't praise the little thief!"

Lucas looked at him confused, "A thief of what?"

"Of information! He stole my IN-FOR-MA-TION! He told me he would help me if I helped him and now he refuses to repay me!"

Lucas rolled his eyes.

"Don't you roll your eyes at me!"

"Don't you tell me what to do."

Xavier looked around, ignoring Lucas. Ian had already gone to class.

"Little bastard creeped out on us, let's go," Xavier said angrily.

Xavier was pissed, and it was payback time. He made sure that Ian wasn't able to hear a word from his teachers. When he tried to look at the board, they clustered in front of his face, it was like trying to look through greasy cellophane. *One day, everyone'll think I'm intermittently deaf and blind*, Ian sighed. Luckily, none of the teachers paid him any attention, and his classmates, still freaked out from Ian writing down their names, stayed as far away from him as possible.

History class finally came. Mr. Griffin came in, his usual smile and happy persona was replaced with heavy sighs and a look of disappointment. Ian could barely hear what he was saying, he caught tiny snippets, something like: "Horrible…next test…study…extra work…."

Mr. Griffin went through the row of chairs, handing each student their test and making a small comment. He reached Ian and seemed reluctant to hand him his test. Ian grabbed it from him and saw a red A+ at the top of his page. He didn't realize he was holding his breath this whole time, until he let it out. Mr. Griffin stared at him; he was saying something about the test: "Congrats…only…perfect score…not…cheating." Again, Ian could only hear pieces because of Xavier and his cohorts screaming in his face.

Mr. Griffin continued to look at Ian, as if waiting for a response, but Ian had no idea what to say. Finally, his teacher moved on, handing out the other tests, obviously not too happy with Ian's score.

Ian didn't care, he smiled at Xavier. He wrote: *Thank you, your screaming actually made me concentrate harder, my best test score ever. Too bad one of your literate friends will have to read this to you.* He finished his message with a smiley face.

"What's he writing?" hissed Xavier.

Lucas hovered over Ian's desk and burst into a fit of laughter. "He said your yelling helped him concentrate, and that he got a perfect score…and it's too bad," Lucas stopped to take an imaginary breath, "that you're illiterate." In unison, the ghosts' eyes flew open wide, filling the room with oohs!

Xavier looked at Ian, his eyes filled with hate. "You'll pay, Mr. Stanley," he spit out the word Stanley. "You'll pay."

Ian yawned, grabbed a pencil, and pretended to poke holes in Xavier. "Whatever," said Ian coolly, not about to let Xavier ruin his moment.

Xavier was determined to make Ian's life a living hell. When recess came, Xavier and his friends surrounded Ian's head like a misty cloud, making it hard for Ian to see where he was going. Recess consisted of him bumping into students. His classmates yelled at him to watch where he was going, and then—those same classmates—ran away, terrified when they realized who they'd just snapped at.

He had just crashed into his third column when he felt someone grab his hand and began pulling him. He squinted through the ghosts surrounding his head, *Oh great, Madison*. Her mouth was moving—as always—but he couldn't make out what she was saying.

He felt her tug downward on his hand, guiding him down safely onto a bench. She sat alongside him, pressing her shoulder into his. "This is going to be a real problem when you start driving," she joked.

"Gross," Ian exclaimed. He pushed himself away from her and fell to the ground with an "oof"—not realizing that he was at the end of the bench. Ian jumped to his feet, embarrassed and angry. Madison's laughter joined in with the ghosts.

"You're so silly," she smiled, grabbing his hand and pulling him back onto the bench. "Listen, I'm only sitting next to you like this so you can hear me. You were swaying and wobbling like you were drunk. Ian Stanley, can you hear me?!"

Ian nodded. He wasn't happy that she was squashed up against him and yelling. It was a three-person bench. He could only imagine what everyone was thinking.

Through his blurred vision, Ian could see teachers and students watching them closely. Most of the kids quickly turned away when they saw him look their way— however, one of the teachers seemed to thrive on confrontation. Ian could barely make out who it was. He just knew it was a woman with long straight hair, striding determinedly toward them.

He couldn't hear what the woman was saying, even though she stood three feet from them. She crossed her arms, so she must be fussing. Madison did all the talking.

"Hi Mrs. Fernandez…. Of course not…. He's dizzy and I'm helping…. If we were…. I would've been kissing him not yelling…."

Ian facepalmed. The ghosts began oohing and wooing singing *The K-I-S-S-I-N-G Song*.

Madison giggled at Ian's reaction. She turned back to their teacher. "Yes…. I think he'll be fine…. I'll look after him…." She looked at Ian, "She's asking if you want to go home!"

"I'll be fine," Ian answered quickly, not wanting to explain to his parents that he'd been sent home for blurred vision and the inability to hear. Going to see a doctor was the last thing he needed.

Madison and Mrs. Fernandez exchanged a few more words, and then she walked away.

Madison looked at him and smiled feeling victorious, but then frowned. "Sorry you're not feeling well!" she yelled again. "What are they doing?!"

"Screaming and surrounding me so I can't see through all of them," he explained.

"You pissed them off?!" she asked, confused but interested.

Ian smiled and nodded, which enraged Xavier, who swore and yelled out all the ways he wanted Ian to suffer and die.

Madison nodded. Ian could feel she was swinging her legs under the bench. "Do you think they have unfinished business?"

The ghosts exploded with laughter. "Did you hear what she said? Oh! I bet she watched *Casper*!" They all started singing Casper's theme song at the top of their lungs. "Casper, the friendly ghost. The friendliest ghost you know...."

Ian shrugged and, out of spite, replied, "I'm not sure if you would call it unfinished business...they are here for a reason, and if they don't discover the reason, they eventually disappear, as if they never existed. Poof."

"Poof?" Madison looked quizzically at Ian.

Ian didn't answer. The ghosts had grown silent. He could hear the birds chirping, his classmates talking, but it was short lived. Xavier rallied his troops.

"Scream as if your life depended on it," Xavier shouted, ignoring the irony…since they were already dead.

"Cyclone," shouted another ghost.

Ian's face grew pale. Cyclone meant that the ghost would spin around Ian's head at a high speed, completely blurring his vision. Ian felt dizzy and nauseous, his vision a continuous semi-transparent blur. He squinted trying to focus on one point, but it was impossible. He closed his eyes, but for some reason, that made him feel worse. He leaned forward, placing his head between his knees.

"Xavier," Ian growled, "has anyone else ever seen you?"

"What?" Xavier threw up his hand silencing the other ghosts.

"In over two hundred years," Ian said icily, "has anyone ever seen you except for me?"

Xavier looked at Ian confused, he felt that he was being led into a trap.

"You don't have to answer, I already know. You and your friends think it's so funny to make my life miserable…, but you know, and I know," said Ian, his eyes darkening, "you need me…and some day, I bet your friends will need me too."

Xavier was silent, he looked toward his friends to see how they were responding.

"I also find it interesting that you've made yourself the boss, the leader, when many of your friends committed heinous crimes far worse than yours.... You ask for a favor, and they all throw themselves at your feet...to do your bidding, as if you're their king," Ian spat.

Xavier gasped. "Don't listen to him!" he yelled, "He's trying to manipulate you!"

"Really?" Ian sneered. "Have I ever lied to you?" he directed his question to Xavier's friends. "You think Xavier's going to help you? He's only concerned about himself."

"No one cares what you think," scoffed Xavier. "I said *no one*," he screamed, as some of the ghosts began flying away. "Come back here you miserable cowards," Xavier shouted.

"Ian?" Madison asked excitedly. "You mean there is a hierarchy among ghosts?" she asked excitedly. "Like some are more powerful than others?"

Ian knew he had everyone's rapt attention. "Not really, there are ghosts like Xavier who would like you to believe that they are all powerful, but they resort to tricks that are little more than just temper tantrums. I call them disruptors...and fools."

"Disruptors? You mean they can't actually hurt you or touch you at all?"

"No, it's all a pitiful charade. They know I'm the *only* one who can communicate with them, who can help them. So, they have to be careful. Like, what if they made me fall and break my neck? Or what if they caused me to step in front of a car? They would have no one else to connect them to the living world. Xavier knows that, and he's just using the others."

"That's it!" Mary the Sloth threw her hands up in resignation. "I'm out of here."

"No don't goooo!" Xavier panicked. "This is what he does. You're letting him get his way!"

"It's not worth it, this is pointless, and he's only targeting you," Lucas told Xavier. He floated away without a backward glance.

Xavier threw a tantrum and cursed Ian. "You stupid little…."

"Give it up, Xavier," Ian interrupted him, "You lost this round."

Madison stared at Ian, fascinated. She'd just experienced what it was like to see Ian talking to ghosts. She'd even learned one of their names. She jumped up off the bench, and spun facing Ian. "I have a gazillion questions!" she gushed.

Ian threw up his hands, "You don't have to yell anymore; most of them left."

"Oh…," Madison breathed. "How did you anger…um… Xavier?"

Xavier stopped yelling for a moment and hovered, listening. Another living being had spoken his name.

"I didn't even know you could do that," she continued. "Can everyone anger ghosts or is it just you because you can communicate with them?"

"I'm pretty sure I'm the only one…I mean that can purposely anger them. I'm sure there are other situations where ghosts see humans do stupid things…and I'm guessing that's got to be frustrating to them, especially if they *like* the person."

Madison was about to hit him with another flurry of questions when she noticed his mood changing. "I'm sorry, I just got really excited," she exclaimed. "I've just got a couple more questions and then I won't ask any more I promise."

"Okay," sighed Ian, "but that's it."

"I was wondering…since they're here, in the school, can they go anywhere else?"

Xavier listened intently.

"They can go wherever they want. Some of them like to venture around, but most of the time they like to stick with a certain place or person."

"A person?"

Ian could hear the uncertainty in her voice.

"What do you mean by that?" she asked.

"For example, there's a ghost named Peter the Lecher. He likes to watch a particular woman."

"Why would the ghost watch her for? You mean, are they related?"

"No, not that I know of," he answered matter-of-factly. "He just likes to spy on her. He watches her all day, all night, except for when he comes to see me every evening to talk about her."

"He watches her even in the bathroom?" she whispered.

He looks at her dully, "Even in the bathroom."

Madison's eyes filled with horror. "You…you have to come over to my house and make sure I'm not being watched. Maybe you can piss them off somehow and make them stop watching…," she stopped herself, realizing she had just announced her worst fears to the ghosts around her.

"You can't get rid of them. And, isn't it better that you don't know? If I told you there were ghosts watching you…."

Madison began to shake.

"Look," he said, suddenly feeling sorry for her, "I doubt any of them are interested in watching *you*, they've got more important things to do."

Madison's mouth dropped in disapproval; she was about to retaliate, but then she shrugged. Ian was right, it was best to appear uninteresting. The more boring, the better.

Chapter 8

Ian's speech had worked. He had actually been able to pay attention in class and take some notes. He felt…well almost normal. Madison appeared at his locker and handed him a fistful of photocopied notes. "Thanks," Ian replied, placing the notes in his backpack, and grabbing the books he needed that night for homework.

"Do you mind if I walk home with you and go to your house for a little while?" Madison asked somewhat awkwardly.

Ian looked at her. *She's up to something*, he thought, *she's never asked to walk home with me.*

"Woooo so romantic," exclaimed Xavier, laying atop the row of lockers, his chin in his hands, kicking his feet. He reached out in front of him and pretended to pick a flower. "She loves me." He plucked off an imaginary petal. "She loves me not," he made a pouty face. "She loves me…. She loves me not…. She loves me!" he shouted. He threw the made-up petalless flower up in the air, and swooped down, grabbing Madison in an embrace.

Ian shook his head, "I'm sorry Madison. I don't think it's a good idea, plus I got tons of homework."

"Oh, come *on*. It's only for a bit."

"Why?" he eyed her suspiciously.

"I'll do some homework there, and help you catch up."

"You already gave me your notes."

"It's the *least* you could do," Madison begged. "Please."

"No. You're just curious and all you'll do is cause trouble," he said firmly.

"For five minutes?" she held up her hand with her five fingers spread out, as if he wouldn't understand what she just asked for.

"I said no. I have to go now."

Madison looked crestfallen, her shoulders fell…. She'd felt a connection with Ian today…. She felt they had shared something…something incredible.

Ian paused. He didn't want to get Madison caught up in his problems. People liked her. Teachers liked her. If she was seen hanging around with him more and more…. He felt horrible. "Thank you for the notes, Madison. I'll see you tomorrow."

His footsteps echoed hollowly in the corridor—just like his heart—as he turned to leave.

Madison stood at his locker, watching him leave.

Ian felt disgusted and frustrated. *Why did I have to tell Madison about the ghosts? Why am I such an idiot? I can't let her come over my house, what if my parents hear her talking about ghosts? They're going to send me to a shrink for sure…and if they talk to my teachers….* For the first time in a long time, Ian let silent tears stream down his face. He hadn't wanted this burden, this pain. He never asked for it, yet it had chosen him, and he was doomed to carry the weight on his shoulders forever.

Ian got home and went through an uneventful family dinner, answering his parents' questions on autopilot. He felt numb. He scraped his food into the trash, and had just started to wash the dishes, when he heard the doorbell.

Everyone stared at the door, then at the clock and then at each other in confusion. "Are we expecting someone?" his mom asked, cleaning her mouth with her napkin, getting ready for their visitor.

His dad shrugged. "Not that I can remember…," he replied with a mouthful of hamburger.

"Not me either," John replied.

The doorbell rang again. "I'll get it," Amy jumped up, eager to see who's actually at the door.

"No!" Tracy snapped her finger at her and pointed at her chair so Amy would sit back down. "I'll get it. You're not supposed to open the door to strangers."

"Neither should you," Amy said under her breath, sitting back down.

Tracy gave her a disapproving stare. Amy immediately dropped her head and concentrated on eating quietly.

In a flash of anger, Ian threw the sponge into the sink, splashing water all over himself and the kitchen floor. "Madison," he hissed. He could hear the ghost wooing at the front door.

Ian's mom looked through the peephole. A young girl with a bright pink hat stood on the porch. *A girl scout?* she wondered. She unbolted the lock and opened the door.

"Hello, Mrs. Stanley!" a girl's voice chirped. "Wow! You look just like Ian! It's great to make your acquaintance," Madison held out her hand to shake Tracy's.

"Uh," Tracy shook it, "I'm so sorry. I didn't realize Ian was having a friend come over. I would've prepared some dinner for you."

"Oh no, no, no, no," Madison threw her hands up shaking them. "I've already eaten, thank you so much! I just came over to study that's all." She gave the toothiest smile she could.

"Of course, of course! Come on in," Ian's mom said, opening the door further to let her enter.

Madison strolled in wearing an ensemble that included every color of the rainbow and then some. An obnoxiously pink hat covered her disheveled hair. She looked like she'd been in a fight with a wind tunnel and lost. Twice. She had on a yellow shirt, under a coral-colored 3/4 sleeve hoodie, and camouflage baggy pants. She looked at the family at the dinner table and waved. Through the doorway she could see Ian standing at the kitchen sink.

"Is that your girlfriend?" Amy shouted to Ian.

"Absolutely not," Ian snapped.

"Don't be so mean, Ian. I'm not *that* ugly," she giggled, then turned to the family. "Hello, I'm Madison. I'm Ian's classmate," she bowed her head slightly. "Namaste."

"Hi, Madison," Ian's father responded. "I'm Ben, a generally quiet, but cool dad, and this is John and Amy…no comment," he smiled, gesturing toward his children.

"Nice to meet you all," she smiled widely. "I love your Jumanji hoodie," Madison said pointing at John.

"Hey Madison, you're not carrying much in that backpack," Amy said matter-of-factly. "What are you supposed to be studying?"

"Amy Stanley!" Tracy fussed, unhappy with Amy questioning their guest.

Madison laughed uneasily. "It's okay, Mrs. Stanley. I didn't bring my books since Ian already has his here, I just brought my notebook."

Ian couldn't believe Madison's audacity. He'd told her she couldn't come over…but she came anyways. Then to top it off, she was lying to his family. He felt betrayed.

Frederick the Scorcher reveled in Ian's frustration. He danced around the dinner table and then flew directly up to Madison's face, standing nose to nose with her. "Oooh," he squealed clapping his hands, "a newcomer, a newcomer! Yep," he confirmed, "definitely a newcomer. I've never seen this one before. Big eyes, firm shoulders, aha, and look at those pants! Her hat says let's go to Hawaii while her pants are saying, no, let's go to war." Frederick hurled himself onto the table laughing.

"Ian," Frederick yelled flying into the kitchen, "is that your girlfriend? Is she evil? She has a weird smile! What's up with her clothes?"

"You said you came over to study?" asked Tracy, walking over toward the dinner table.

"Yes, if you don't mind," Madison laughed nervously.

"Of course not!" Tracy smiled. "Honestly, I'm pleasantly surprised. This is a first for us. Ian usually prefers to study alone, and he didn't mention anything, so we really weren't expecting company."

Ian watched Madison's ears burn red. He remained in the kitchen, watching to see how everything would play out.

"Oh," Madison laughed, "silly Ian. He must have forgotten to tell you. We study together in school all the time. I just think he's a little shy," she giggled winking at Ian's mom. "Mind if we go study?"

"Of course not! Please go ahead. Ian's in the kitchen washing his dishes," Tracy smiled, and sat back down next to Ben, looking pleased.

"Great!" Madison smiled, excusing herself.

"Good luck!" Ben yelled.

"Hi Ian," Madison chimed, smiling broadly.

"What are you doing here?" Ian asked hotly. He ripped a paper towel from the roll and wiped up the water from the floor.

"I'm here to help you study."

"I don't need help studying. So you can leave now. I asked you not to come, and you came over anyways. Not cool."

"But I *do* need to study," she shifted uneasily from one foot to the other and turned her head down. "I promise. It'll be quick. It's not much."

"How did you even find my house? Did you follow me from school?"

Madison was at the point of tears. She knew his family could hear them talking, since all that separated them was a half wall. "Please Ian," she whispered. "I'll never show up uninvited again, I promise."

"Oh?" Ian raised his left brow. "So if we *study* today, you won't bother me ever again?"

Madison's jaw dropped in surprise. "I do so much for you. I never mean to bother you. I consider you my friend. This is just who I am. Can't you accept that?"

Ian watched her eyes start to water. "Don't cry," he snapped. He shook his head angrily, "this is never going to happen again. Agreed?"

Madison's heart leapt. She smiled broadly and nodded vigorously. "Yes, sir!" she saluted him.

It didn't matter how mean Ian was to Madison, for some reason, she still lingered around. She had so many opportunities to have much better friends, yet she preferred to be around him. Hence, Ian suspected she was only interested in him for one reason and one reason alone…the ghosts.

Ian headed for the stairs without a word. Madison followed close behind him.

"Going to go study now!" Madison cheerfully told his parents.

"Okay, have fun," Tracy smiled.

Ben cleared his throat, "Yup, study...uh...well," not knowing what to say.

Madison followed Ian up the stairs into his bedroom. He closed the door, leaving it open a crack. Xavier, Helga and Frederick went crazy, bombarding Ian with questions. He ignored them and plopped onto his bed, leaving Madison standing by his desk.

"Cool room," Madison said looking around.

Ian filled his lungs and then released the world's longest annoyed sigh. "Why are you here? Really."

"Love, you fool!" screamed Xavier. "I can see it in her eyes!"

"It's true," added Helga, "she's infatuated."

Madison looked around his room, hoping she would catch a glimpse of a ghost. She squinted, turning slowly.

"What are you doing?" Ian asked, growing impatient.

"I was hoping that once I was in your room, I'd be able to see the ghost too." She dropped her backpack on the floor and sat on his desk chair.

"That's why you're here? To use me to try to see ghosts?"

"No, no," insisted Madison, "I just thought, you know, while I'm here, why not at least try to see them."

Ian sat quietly, staring at her, tapping his finger on his bed, his anger building.

"Fine, I want to talk to the guy who's spying on the woman."

"What?" Ian asked, not sure he'd heard her correctly.

"I just want to speak to him, that's all," she said quickly. "Is he here?"

"No. Why do you want to talk to him? He's a horrible person."

"I think I'd feel better if I speak my mind."

"You came here just to talk to *him*?" he asked incredulously.

Ian saw that she was trembling. *Is she afraid of me?* he wondered, *or of speaking to Peter?*

"Ye-yes," she stuttered. "I'll leave after I talk to him. You said he comes every evening, right?"

Ian nodded, "Yes, but he hasn't come yet."

"Do you mind if I study until he does? I won't bother you, and I don't want to lie to your parents." She pulled her notebook out of her bag before Ian could tell her no.

"Listen Madison, my family doesn't know that I can see or talk to ghosts. If they find out…."

"I kind of figured; that's why I lied to your parents. I'm sorry about that. I'll just sit here and quietly work on my homework, and if you would," she smiled softly, "let me know when he arrives."

"Madison, if they hear you talking to an *imaginary person*, I'm the one that's gonna pay the price. I live here, you don't. They're going to wind up sending me to a shrink or worse. Is that what you want?" he whispered angrily.

"They won't hear me. I'll speak quietly, and if they do, I'll just pretend to be acting, like we're working on a presentation. Ian, I *promise* I won't get you into any trouble."

"Why don't you just tell me what you want to say, and I'll tell him when I see him?"

"No offense, but I really just need to say it. I know that you hate talking to them, and this way, I can just say what I came to say, and be done with it. I promise it won't take long and as soon as I'm done, I'll leave."

"Fine!" he whispered, exasperated. "Suit yourself."

Madison gave him a weak smile and placed her notebook on the desk, so she could work on her English homework while she waited.

"Oh, you never answered me. How did you find me?" Ian asked.

Madison looked at him and smiled. "I have mad detective skills that I'd like to keep to myself."

"You owe me!" he fussed.

"Fine!" she surrendered. "I searched you up in a phonebook. We still get those in the mail. Took some trial and error, but there aren't that many Stanleys in this town."

"You went to every Stanley's house?" Ian asked in disbelief.

"Well not *every* one of them. I found yours on the third try."

"Why didn't you just call?"

"So you wouldn't tell me off on the phone…," she answered.

"Well, I'm sure you annoyed a lot of people."

"I don't care. I'm used to it," she smiled at him.

"Not surprised," he mumbled.

"At least your mom looks like you," she explained. "Otherwise she would've probably been weirded out if I came over asking if you live here."

"I think she was weirded out that you came either way, especially alone."

"It's a safe town. My parents don't worry too much."

"Still…. Alright," he sighed, "I'm doing my homework now."

Madison nodded, and went back to hers.

Ian leaned over the side of his bed and fished his homework and a mechanical pencil out of his backpack. He grabbed his headphones. *Ah silence, at last.* He stood a pillow upright against the wall and leaned back on it and rested his binder on his thighs. Ian flipped to his English section and read the question he was to address in his essay.

What is the most interesting experience you've ever had? Write about what happened and describe how you felt during and after the event. *Yeah right, I'll just make up something.*

Ian was deep into his essay when Peter arrived. Ian glanced at his clock; he'd been writing for nearly forty-five minutes.

"Ian, you wouldn't believe what I just went through with Melody, there was ano…," he stopped midsentence, noticing Madison sitting at Ian's desk, working away. "Oh, but what have we here?! A visitor!" he exclaimed excitedly.

Ian had seen Peter coming and told Madison, "He's here." He took off his headphones, intrigued as to what was about to happen.

Madison jumped. "Oh my goodness! You scared me," she breathed. She began trembling again. "So, uh, what's his name?"

"Peter," Ian muttered.

"Oh my! She came to visit me?!" Peter was unbelievably ecstatic. "What does she want? Is she a relative of mine and I never knew?"

Xavier was filled with jealousy, "Pfft. Doubt it, you're butt ugly, and she's somewhat pleasant to look at."

"Look who's talking," Helga laughed.

"Shut up, Porky!" Xavier fumed.

Madison quickly went to the door, turned the knob and closed it quietly, so Ian's family couldn't overhear. "Where is he? I want to face him."

"He's standing right beside you, by the lamp."

Madison breathed in, filling her lungs, she closed her eyes and balled her hands into fists. "Peter," she said in a low voice, "what you're doing is absolutely disgusting. You're a disgrace. Spying on women is wrong in so many ways. How would *you* feel if that happened to you? It's incredibly immoral. Is this how your parents brought you up? How dare…."

She came here for this? thought Ian dumbstruck. *Oh dear God.* He couldn't take it. He put his headphones on and went back to his homework, hoping she would be done soon.

Peter looked from Ian, to Xavier, to Helga and then back to Madison. "Oh my! This one's feisty," he broke out laughing.

"You tell him, Madison," shouted Helga. "About time someone put you in your place, Peter."

Ian glanced over at Madison. She was jabbing her finger at Peter, her face bright red. He caught little snippets about his obscene behavior and that he should be ashamed.

Peter yawned and *sat* beside Ian on his bed. "Ian my boy, you've got quite the interesting gal there. I would hate to be that lamp."

Madison of course thought she was still fussing at Peter and didn't realize she was telling Ian's lamp off.

"Thanks for the freak show, it made my day. I'll have to visit her when she gets older."

"You'll do no such thing," Ian whispered coldly, slamming his pencil down on his homework. "If you ever want anything from me…."

"Whoa boy, whoa," Peter said, holding up his hands in surrender. "Easy, I get it, and I respect it, hands off. We cool?"

Ian nodded angrily. Even *he* was surprised at his own reaction. He wasn't sure why Peter's comment had angered him so much.

"Okay, I've got to go anyways. Melody has a stalker, can you believe that? Please tell your little friend that I don't have time to stay here and listen...besides, I'm dead. But you can probably convince her to give the stalker an earful, there still might be hope for his soul. I'm off," Peter declared and floated away.

Madison was *still* going. She jabbed her finger toward the lamp.

"He left," Ian told her.

"What?! He can't leave. I hadn't finished!" she complained.

Ian shrugged. "He went back to spying. But he did say he was amused by your performance."

"I didn't come to *entertain* him," she snarled.

"Aha," he dismissed her comment. "Well, you're never going to change him. I think you're done here, right?"

Ian hopped off his bed and padded over to the door. As soon as he twisted the knob, the door swung open, banging into the wall. John and Amy fell onto the floor in a heap.

"Ow, you moron, get off of me," Amy yelled, her mouth stuck like glue to the floor. John rolled away from her.

Ian felt blood drain from his face. He felt sick. *What did they hear?* "What are you doing?!" he screamed.

"You think this is funny? You think eavesdropping is funny? Good to know, because from now on you can count on me hanging out by *your* doors and listening in on the conversations you're having with your friends."

Madison's heart skipped a beat when he mentioned the word *friends*.

Amy sat up, shocked, "You wouldn't dare!"

"You just wait. Tit for tat," he yelled. He heard his parents running up the stairs.

"What's going on here?" Ben asked, looking from Ian to John and Amy.

Amy and John's eyes widened.

"What are you doing on the floor? Were you spying on them?!" Ian's mom yelled.

"Of course not," John answered innocently, "I just fell on Amy."

Amy pointed an accusatory finger at Ian, "He's spying on some woman!"

"What?" Tracy exclaimed, looking at Ian.

"Can't you tell she's lying?" Ian responded coolly. "She's trying to put blame on me so that you don't punish *them* for eavesdropping."

"That is *not* true!" Amy yelled. "First of all, you're not allowed to close your door when you have company. House rules." She looked to her parents for confirmation.

They stood silently, listening. "And secondly, you *are* spying on someone. I heard Madison say so!"

"Well Amy, you just confirmed that you *were* eavesdropping…," Ben sighed.

"Oh," Madison said calmly, "but I wasn't talking about Ian at all. If you'd actually listened carefully and not rushed to a conclusion, you would've understood that I was just acting. It's part of our school play."

"About spying on women?" John asked suspiciously. "And why would the door be closed, unless you were hiding something?"

"I closed the door so I wouldn't disturb any of you. Plus, it's not like I'm comfortable with everyone listening to me rehearse. This is a big deal for me, I've never been able to perform in public, and Ian is one of the few people that has ever supported me," Madison sighed. "I shouldn't have closed the door. I obviously made a mistake, and I apologize, it was my fault."

"Well, it didn't sound like you were acting to me," Amy said bluntly. "You were directing your comments to someone. I'm not dumb."

"Okay," breathed Madison, now getting agitated at Amy's accusations. "If I may?" she asked addressing Ian's parents.

Tracy nodded her head for her to continue.

"I know Ian pretty well, and he's an honorable kid," Madison started. "Plus, I know that Ian basically goes to school, and then comes straight home. And," she offered, "if you look out of Ian's window, all you can see is trees. Are you trying to say that in the short amount of time it takes him to walk to and from school, he is spying on someone? The answer you're looking for is no."

"He leaves the house extra early," Amy said, shaking her head matter-of-factly. "Plenty of time in the morning to spy and then head to school."

"So do I. Now I guess you're going to accuse me of the same thing. I arrive extra early to school just about every morning, and who do I always find there studying? Your brother."

"Fine," Amy started, a devious smile spreading across her face. "Madison, why don't you recite your lines, I'm sure we'd all love to hear them."

"That's enough!" Tracy interrupted. "Amy, John, go to my room. Now! Ian, you know the rules, when you have company, your door *stays* open, no exceptions. You're off the hook for now since this is your first visitor and I trust you."

Amy and John began protesting. "Go now!" Tracy yelled, then turned to Madison. "I'm sorry about this. I never would've thought they'd be so disrespectful. We do have a rule for keeping the doors open when there's a guest in the room, but thank you for standing up for Ian, you're more than welcome to come over whenever you want, if you're okay with dealing with sibling rivalry that is," she smiled. Ian's face fell when his mom said *whenever you want.*

Madison gasped, delighted, "Thank you, Mrs. Stanley."

"Ahem, yes, uh, sorry about that," Ian's father added. "Madison, it's getting dark outside. I'm going to give you a ride home."

Madison looked at the clock behind her, "8:07!" she exclaimed. "You're right. I better get going!"

"Alright," Ben smiled, heading toward the stairs. "Ian, you coming?"

"That's okay, I have to...," Ian started.

"It wasn't really a yes or no question. Put your jacket on," his dad said firmly.

The five-minute car ride to Madison's house was quick and uneventful. On the way back to their house, Ian's dad told him that he was impressed with Madison, and the fact that she had stood up for him so furiously. He reiterated that she was welcome back at any time. Ian listened quietly, wishing the day would end.

Chapter 9

The next day at recess, Madison plopped herself next to Ian.

"Is this going to be an everyday thing? You're not going to be able to hang out with the cool kids if you keep hanging out with me," he explained his voice filled with sarcasm.

"You're so funny." She banged her shoulder into his, nearly knocking him off the bench. "I didn't get you into any trouble, did I? Did they suspect anything?"

"I don't think so, but yes, you did make my life a lot more difficult."

"Oh," she said. "I'm sorry. Quick question," she said, ignoring his salty comment. "How many of the ghosts are women?"

"Hmm," he'd never thought of counting them. He cocked his head. "About 20 to 30 percent…, I guess."

She nodded. "You know," she looked down, "I was wrong, about you having a gift…you know, to be able to see ghosts. I thought about it a lot last night. It's not like you're getting anything out of them. If it weren't for them, you would have a normal life, with lots of friends," she paused, thinking things through. "It's of course, much easier for me, I can't see nor hear them. I could even choose not to believe you can speak with them if I wanted to. But I don't. I know it's real. Ian, I can't even imagine what it would be like to be you." She pulled a small notebook out of her hoodie.

"In all fairness," she continued, "I'm ashamed to say, that I've been watching you for months and…," her face fell, "writing about you. I've observed the way you treated people, your idiosyncrasies. You see, I thought that if a person was brought up in a hostile environment surrounded by evil…that the person would at some point…*become* evil. But I can see the good in you. You're nothing like them. Sure, you're antisocial, you're usually angry, and it's like you have this negative energy surrounding you…, but you're not evil at all. I can tell…that, you're good."

Madison pulled the papers from her notebook and tore them to shreds. "I don't need these anymore," she smiled putting her hand on his shoulders. "I think I've figured out why I'm drawn to you," she exclaimed happily. "I believe I was sent here to save you."

"Huh?" blurted Ian, finally breaking his silence.

"What if all of this was a test?" she said bobbing up and down on the bench. "Maybe it's like in that Christmas movie where the guy could see the ghosts, and each of them showed him how horrible his life would be if he didn't change. Maybe you're that guy! Ian you need to decide if you're going to…."

The bell rang. Ian sighed with relief, jumping to his feet. Recess was over.

"Wait, hear me out," Madison called out to him, as he walked away from her. She jogged alongside him, "You can probably have a sort of, necromancer job," she went on. "I'm not bothering you, am I?"

"Madison, I appreciate your psychoanalysis of me, I really do…but enough is enough okay?"

"I was just trying to help," she entered the classroom and slid into her desk in front of him.

"Just help, less," Ian sighed. "Please."

School seemed to drag on longer than usual and when the bell for dismissal rang, Ian found himself racing through the hallway to the door. He didn't stop running until he was back home. He just wanted to be left alone. Unfortunately, as he climbed the stairs to his room, he noticed Peter was already there, pacing back and forth frantically. "Ian! Ian! You're home. You have to do something!" he exclaimed wringing his hands.

Ian shut his door and leapt onto his bed. He grabbed the remote and powered on his television. He flicked through the channels until he found *Teletubbies*. Everyone went insane! Xavier cursed Ian, then cursed Peter for pushing Ian's buttons. Helga yelled at both of them for their idiocy. They all turned on each other, and then pleaded with Ian: "Please, turn it off!"

"Ian," Xavier pleaded, "Peter's been watching that woman for too long! You have to get rid of him. He's disgusting."

"Hey, speak for yourself," Peter fumed and turned to Ian, "Xavier makes your life miserable…you can't even concentrate. At least I'm dignified and respectful."

"Are you listening to me?" howled Xavier. "Ian!"

Ian grabbed the remote and raised the volume on the television. "Leave me alone, or this is what you'll get every day and every night."

Peter threw his arms up in surrender and left, mumbling under his breath, leaving Xavier and Helga behind.

Ian had to admit, it was unusual for Peter to be riled up. He was usually calm and collected. *Well*, he sighed, *suits him right for spying, he's finally suffering the consequences.*

Peter never came back that evening which Ian thought was odd. *He must really be worried about that stalker.* Helga and Xavier decided to leave Ian alone, and entertain themselves with a boo competition.

"Alright," Xavier declared, "whoever can say boo the longest while they wiggle their bodies like this," he floated about a foot above the floor and wiggled, "is the winner."

"Oh, oh, oh, count me in," Frederick said joining Xavier and Helga.

The three ghosts lined up in front of Ian's clock. "I'm going to hold up three fingers," Xavier instructed. "When the last finger drops, initiate booing and gyrating."

"Are you sure you can count that high?" Helga snickered.

"Har, har, har." Xavier thrust out his hand, holding up three fingers, then two, then one. As soon as the last finger dropped, the ghosts began booing and gesticulating in earnest. Helga dropped out first because she couldn't stop laughing at Frederick and Xavier's gyrations.

Helga cheered them on. "Xavier, you're full of hot air, you should definitely win. Frederick, look at you, you're turning a beautiful shade of green!"

Finally, Xavier couldn't take it anymore. He bent over, his hands on his knees, gasping for…air? "He's a cheat. He's a cheat," Xavier yelled, pointing a shaky finger at Frederick.

"I didn't cheat!" Frederick looked shocked. "How dare you accuse me of cheating! Helga," he turned to her for support.

"I saw you take a breath," Xavier chided. He crossed his arms, "Where's your self-respect? It's impossible to find an honest ghost these days."

"My word," Helga put her hands on her hips and shook her head. "You're both losers," she yawned. "Good night boys, I'm off to take a ghost nap."

"More like eat an entire cake," Xavier snickered.

A week went by without much chaos. Things seemed pretty normal, except for Peter's absence. Ian should have been happy, it was one less ghost after all, but he couldn't stop his mind from wondering what happened.

Xavier and Helga couldn't decide what to make of it either. One day they would be fussing at Ian for chasing him away with *Teletubbies*, and the next day they would be congratulating him for getting rid of the weirdo. Both the living and the dead seemed confused as to what his disappearance meant.

For some unexplainable reason, the kids at school appeared to be especially haunted whenever Ian was around. He saw them whispering in the hallways, averting their eyes when he walked by.

"They think you're a demon," Madison said calmly. She was standing in the doorway to the History classroom.

"Great…just what I need to improve my social status," he groaned. "Maybe I should start dragging a dead cat around too, you know, just to complete the image."

"A hockey mask and a chainsaw perhaps," Madison offered.

"Why are they so scared of me now? I mean, they've always whispered behind my back and given me weird looks, but now, they honestly appear frightened."

"Yeah, about that. Remember the day you slipped and fell?"

Ian nodded, recalling the event.

"Then, do you remember several people laughing at you?"

Ian shrugged, "Yeah. Is this going somewhere?"

"Well, Lisa Colby said that you wrote their names in a notebook, and from what she told me, three of the ones that laughed at you got really sick."

"You're kidding me, right? I never wrote down anyone's names, I was just pretending. On top of that, if I had magical powers, I wouldn't waste my time on making people sick."

"I know you would never hurt anyone, but you asked what's going on. Mario broke his leg. Tina got food poisoning. And Cheri is in the hospital getting tested for something. She's been throwing up and suffering from horrible headaches."

"Okay, well, pure coincidence," Ian explained. "But you know that I had nothing to do with that. It's like the Salem Witch Trials all over again."

"Do you think the ghosts could have made them sick?" Madison asked. "You know, to make people think you did it?"

"No," Ian shook his head. "I wish I could blame it on them, but the ghosts can't touch solids. If they could, Xavier would have choked me to death by now. Again…all of this is pure coincidence, we go to a big school with lots of kids…people are bound to get sick."

Madison looked at him and agreed. "Have you heard anything else from Peter? Did he change his ways?"

"I doubt it. I haven't seen him for a long time."

She gasped, "Since when?"

"'Bout a week ago."

Madison beamed. "Really? That's...incredible! Maybe my speech worked!"

Ian scowled at her. "You're not going to change *years* of a psycho's behavior with one impassioned speech."

"I am," she smiled. "You can't tell me you're not happy about that. I told him what's what, and now, he's gone! You don't have to deal with him anymore!"

Ian cocked his head and gave her an annoyed expression. "Are you listening to yourself?"

"Just admit it," she nudged him, as he gave her a nasty face for touching him. "I'm your *hero*," she sang. "Don't worry, you don't have to thank me. So have any of the other ghosts left? Is this the first time this has happened? I could reprimand the others if you'd like."

"No, no, I think you've done enough helping for a while...for a lifetime."

"How is asking questions bothering you?"

"Shh!" Ian hissed. Madison was about to fuss at him for being rude, but then she realized he'd seen something in the hallway.

"What? What is it, what's wrong?" Madison asked, looking at him, "What is it?"

Peter was racing through the hallway at a blinding speed. "It's Peter," Ian whispered.

"Perfect." Madison squared her stance to face off against him. "I didn't get to finish what I had to say last time."

"Ian! Ian!" Peter yelled at the top of his lungs.

"Not now, Peter, I have to go to class."

"Wait! Don't go! Please Ian!" Peter begged him.

Please? Ian froze. He's never said 'please' before.

"He's going to kill her! Ian, the stalker is going to kill Melody! You have to come with me!"

Ian faced Peter at the word 'kill,' feeling blood draining from his face.

"What's up, Ian?" Madison kept asking. "Are you okay?"

"Why are you just staring?!" Peter yelled at him. "Please Ian, I'm begging you, you have to come! Just follow me!"

"I know you want me to get rid of him," Ian replied. "This is only for your benefit, so you could continue watching her, by yourself."

Madison saw the color drain from Ian's face, and grew quiet.

"Of course, that would be wonderful," Peter exclaimed, "but it's not that. The man that is stalking her, he has a knife...." He burst into tears. "I know what it's like to be stabbed to death, Ian," he sobbed. "I don't want her to go through that horror. I'm begging you," he yelled, his entire body trembling uncontrollably.

"Okay, okay, I believe you, Peter. What's her address? I'll call the cops," he decided, and turned toward the school office.

"No!!!! There's no time! They probably won't even believe you...! Ian! Please, she's going to die if we don't hurry!"

"Ugh!" Ian stopped running and hit his hands on his thighs in exasperation.

Madison was becoming agitated now, after hearing the word 'cops.' "What's going *on*, Ian? Tell me! Come on!"

"What's her address?" Ian pressed, "The cops can be there much faster than I can!"

"I don't know! I don't know. She only lives a couple of blocks away! We need to go now!" Peter screamed at him.

"Fine," Ian yelled. "Lead the way," unsure how he was going to stop a man with a knife.

Peter nodded vigorously and floated as fast as he could out of the school. Ian tore through the hallway, right behind him.

"Ian! Ian Stanley!" Madison yelled, "Where are you going?"

A teacher stepped into the hallway. "Get over here, young lady, now!"

Madison looked down the hallway, Ian was just pushing through the main school doors. Another teacher stepped into the hall to see what all of the commotion was about. Madison turned and gave them a defiant look and took off running after Ian.

Ian dodged and darted through pedestrians down the busy sidewalk, unaware that Madison was rapidly closing the distance between them as she chased behind him.

"Watch out!" Madison screamed.

Ian slid to a stop, just as a truck screeched in front of him. "Watch it kid!" the driver snapped.

Ian ignored the man and sprinted off again, adrenaline coursing through his veins. For the first time in his life, he felt that he had a purpose.

"Wait for me!" Madison yelled, panting.

"No, don't wait for her!" Peter screamed. "No time!"

Ian didn't need to be told. He knew that every second counted. He dashed across another road, dodging cars, ignoring the squealing brakes and angry horns.

"Here! Here!" Peter yelled, floating in front of a white house with a red door. "She's home!" he cried pointing at her blue Honda Civic. "She always comes back from work to eat lunch. The guy is hiding in her bedroom closet waiting for her with a knife. You need to tell her!"

Ian bolted up the porch steps. His lungs were burning, he could barely breathe. His heart pounded.

"Hurry up!" Peter yelled at him.

Ian stood on his toes, there was a small window at the top of the door. He could see Melody walking up the stairs…a vision of the man jumping from the closet, stabbing her, seared through his mind's eye.

"Ian, knock!" screamed Peter. "He's going to kill her. Knock on the door! Knock! Knock! KNOCK!"

Ian balled up his fist, and began pounding on the door, screaming Melody's name.

Madison dashed up the steps and grabbed Ian's shoulder. "What are you doing? What's going on?"

Ian pounded on the door furiously. "Melody," he begged, "please open the door."

"She's coming! She's coming!" Peter passed back and forth through the wall.

Ian kept knocking until Melody finally opened the door. "What in the world are you doing?!" she shouted, her face filled with anger. "What's the matter?!" Her face transformed from anger to concern. "Are you hurt?"

Ian's throat tightened, "There's, there's a…." Ian had been close to murderers his entire life, why couldn't he talk now? He could feel his mouth moving, but nothing was coming out.

"Tell her," Peter screamed, "tell her there's a man in her house!"

"What's going on, Ian, why aren't you saying anything?" Madison asked.

Melody looked from Ian to Madison and then back at Ian. "Look kid, I'm on my lunch break, and I only get a little bit of time, so if this is some joke, it's not funny."

"Tell her, you idiot! What are you waiting for?!" Peter screamed.

Ian looked at the beautiful woman in the doorway, he wanted to tell her, that there was a man waiting to kill her, but it was like fear had an icy grip on his vocal cords. "Your room," he gasped finally. He looked at his arm oddly, watching it raise and point. The word 'room' bubbled in his brain as if he was trying to speak underwater.

Melody narrowed her eyes. She turned and looked over her shoulder to where Ian was pointing. "Um, I'm not sure what you're trying to say…. Is he a mute?" she asked Madison.

"No," she shook her head, she was just as confused by his behavior as Melody.

"Okay…do you need me to call an ambulance?"

"No, no, no!" Madison answered abruptly, shaking her hands at her. "I'm so sorry, it's okay. I'll take care of him." She put her hands on Ian's arm, as if protecting him. "He lives nearby. I'll get him home."

Melody nodded slowly, sure that there was more to the story, but she didn't have time to sort things out. "Look, I have to get back to work. Are you sure he's alright?"

"Yes, ma'am," Madison smiled. "Sorry about that. Heading back right now! So sorry."

"Okay…," Melody slowly closed the door, watching Ian, until the door clicked shut.

What's the matter with me? Ian thought. *I've never been so terrified in my entire life. I have to move. I can't let her die!*

"What's going on?" Madison said through clenched teeth. "What were you pointing at? Tell me!"

Peter joined in, "She's going to die because of you, do something!" He disappeared through the door, and then reappeared. "She's going up the stairs, Ian! You have to help her!"

Ian fought back the urge to vomit. Trembling wildly, he stumbled down the porch steps.

"Where are you going?!" Peter was tearing his ghostly hair out of his head. "Go back! Stop! Please," he begged.

Ian's knees buckled. He knelt in the garden beside the porch and grabbed a stone the size of a golf ball.

Peter disappeared through the front door. Seconds later, he returned screaming, "She's going in the room!"

"Ian, what are you doing?" Madison grabbed his arm.

Ian shrugged her away, cocked his arm, and threw the stone at the front window as hard as he could. The rock shattered a large window, flew through the living room, smashing into a large picture frame, sending it crashing to the floor.

Melody came storming down the stairs, screaming. Her face looked like she was ready to murder someone, and that someone, just happened to be Ian Stanley.

Ian couldn't explain it, but as the window shattered, sending glistening shards of glass into the air all around him, his fear vanished. His trembling stopped. He felt powerful. A sudden surge of adrenaline coursed through his veins.

Melody threw the front door open. "You!" she growled, "Stay where you are, I'm calling the police."

Ian charged back up the steps, and shoved Melody aside. She stumbled and crashed into a table.

"Ian," Madison cried out. "What are you doing?"

"Go Ian! Go!" Peter yelled in triumph.

Ian quickly looked around the living room, ignoring all the yelling. He found a blue ceramic lamp and yanked it out of the outlet. He looped the cord around his hand, so he wouldn't trip, and ran up the stairs.

Madison ran over to Melody and helped her to her feet. "Are you okay?"

Peter raced up the stairs ahead of Ian. "He's in here! In here!" He pointed excitedly at Melody's closet.

Ian stared at the closet door, he knew that the stalker was waiting on the other side, ready to pounce. Ian raised the lamp above his head. He inched forward and grabbed the doorknob. He knew as soon as the door opened, his nightmare would begin. He locked his jaw, steeling his nerves, and flung the door open.

A man, dressed completely in black, bolted out of the closet like a crazed animal. Ian smashed the lamp down on his forehead, the lamp shattered into pieces. The stalker screamed, placing a hand over his eye. He whipped his knife through the air, slicing through Ian's hoodie and t-shirt. Ian felt the white-hot pain of the knife's blade as it slashed across his chest.

"Great job, Ian! Keep at it!" Peter cheered. "Get him!"

The stalker held his bloody face with his left hand, stabbing at Ian with his right. Ian fought back, kicking and punching.

Madison raced into the room just in time to see Ian throw himself across Melody's bed, trying to get away from the man's knife. Peter was yelling at Ian, "You've got him on the run, get him, get him!"

Ian threw whatever he could find within arm's reach. Books, shoes, a water bottle, an alarm clock. The man moved in on Ian, cornering him, a sick smile spread across his bloodied face.

He thrust his knife at Ian's face. Ian moved his head just in the nick of time, as the attacker buried his knife to the hilt in the wall where his head had been.

The stalker was so preoccupied with Ian, that he hadn't noticed Madison in the room. She grabbed a snow globe from the windowsill. The stalker faked an attack with his knife, and then drove his foot into Ian's torso. Ian crumbled to the floor, gasping for breath.

"Hey you!" screamed Madison.

The stalker froze for a split second and then wheeled around to face her.

"Leave him alone!" She threw the snow globe like a professional quarterback, striking the man directly on the forehead. He fell back, against the wall and slumped to the floor unconscious.

Melody hobbled into her bedroom, clutching the doorframe. "Wha…," it was her turn to be at a loss for words.

"You did it!" Peter cried out. "Ian, I can't believe you did it."

Ian, fought to stand, he felt light-headed and sick. He smiled weakly at Peter, "She's okay."

Peter flew over to Ian and attempted to hug him. "Thank you, Ian."

Ian shook his head; he could barely see him. "Peter?" Ian called out.

"Thank you," Peter reached out, and put his hand over Ian's. He smiled, and then began to fade away. Ian couldn't tell if he heard the words or imagined them, "Thank you," as Peter vanished without a trace.

Ian rubbed his eyes. Pain rushed through him, causing him to cry out. He looked up at Madison, he could see her rushing toward him, and then he was falling, falling to the ground.

Chapter 10

Ian's eyes flickered open. Everything was white. *Am I in Heaven? What is that beeping sound? Oh*, he thought, seeing the heart monitor. He tried to sit up, but he felt a jabbing pain in his stomach, making him cry out in pain.

"Oh sweetie! Don't get up!" his mom rushed to his side. "How are you feeling?"

Ian looked at his mom, trying to remember how he got there. "Is Melody okay?"

"Yes." She grabbed Ian's bandaged hand gently. "You saved her life."

Ian smiled weakly. "Good," he whispered. He carefully raised his head looking around the room. His entire family was there, staring at him, weird smiles on their faces. He nodded at them, not wanting to speak.

He laid his head back onto his pillow and closed his eyes. He could see Peter's face, hear his voice, and then he vanished...was that all a dream?

"Ian," his mother said softly, "there's someone here to see you."

"Okay," Ian said softly. He wondered why they weren't asking him a million questions about not being at school, and how he wound up at some lady's house, protecting her against an armed assailant. He was surprised when Melody walked in, he was sure it was going to be Madison.

"Hi Ian. How are you feeling?"

Ian looked up into Melody's eyes. They were beautiful. He could see how Peter had fallen in love with her. "I feel like I was run over by a tractor trailer," Ian smiled weakly, "but I'm alright."

Melody smiled and shook her head. "It took a lot of courage to do what you did…and now I understand why you were so afraid."

Ian smiled shyly, remembering the awkward porch moment.

"I just wanted to say thank you for saving my life. I was incredibly rude to you, and you…well you were just trying to help me. You're a brave young man," Melody said, tears filling her eyes. "Thank you." She reached into her pocket and pulled out the rock he had thrown through her window. Ian's face blushed red. She handed him the rock and smiled.

Ian turned the rock in his hands. Melody had painted the word courage on it. Ian's heart soared with pride. "Thank you," he whispered.

Melody thanked Ian's parents and waved goodbye to Ian. He waved, and closed his eyes, falling into a deep sleep.

Ian wound up spending several days in the hospital so the doctors could run a series of tests. He was lucky to be alive. Broken ribs, a concussion and dozens of stitches. The time passed quickly, Ian had quite a few visitors, and as each day passed, his room became more and more cramped.

Madison came by each day and stayed until the nurses kicked her out at night. Melody came by to check on him, as well as Helga, Xavier, Mary, Frederick and so on.

"Did you think you could escape us so easily?" teased Xavier. "There's nowhere you can hide where we won't find you."

"Are you an idiot?" Helga scoffed. "You think he got all of these injuries just to get away from us?"

"Quiet, Chubbers! I wasn't talking to you!"

"Ian," Ronald the Glutton asked, while Helga and Xavier argued. "Have you seen Peter? We haven't seen him since you...well since you wound up here."

Instantly, the room became silent. Everyone turned to Ian waiting for his response.

I guess Peter did vanish, Ian thought. He paused, carefully planning how to respond. "I think that I have figured something out...it seems that I am actually linked to your destiny. You see," he answered, a sly grin forming on his face, "I control your future."

"Is that what happened to Peter?" Helga asked, barely breathing.

"Maybe so," said Ian.

The ghosts turned in unison as Madison entered the room.

"Ugh," moaned Xavier, "not her." He pretended to bash his head against the wall, over and over.

"Hey Ian," said Madison, giving him a huge grin. She plopped into the chair beside him and kicked her feet out. "So, are you ever going to thank me for saving your life?"

"Ooh la la," said Xavier. "Ian, you never told us she was the real hero."

Ian rolled his eyes. "What are you talking about?"

Madison looked shocked. "Are you kidding me, Ian Stanley? If it hadn't been for me, he would have probably killed you. Actually, I'm sure he would have killed you."

"Okay, okay, fine, thank you."

"For…?" asked Madison.

"Ugh," groaned Ian, "for saving my life."

"Ah, now, don't you feel so much better?" cooed Madison.

"Not really, I feel nauseous."

"You're just lovesick, silly boy," giggled Madison.

"Woooooooh," chorused the ghosts.

Ian had to admit, he was happy to be back home. John had even put Ian's arm around his shoulders and helped him up the stairs. Amy had made him a plate of heart-shaped chocolate chip cookies.

He stood in front of his mirror and stared at the reflection of the skinny boy. His hands, arms, and face were still covered in bandages. He pulled up his shirt, his entire torso was tightly wrapped to protect his ribs. He gazed into his gray eyes, disappearing into another world, where memories and—

"Would you get over yourself?" Xavier scoffed. "You're not home two minutes and you're gawking at yourself in the mirror. My God."

Ian watched as a smile appeared on his face.

"Did you see that? Did you see that?" asked Xavier. "Helga, I believe I actually made him smile. Someone who knows how to spell, write this down. I need the date and the time, and a photograph."

Ian pulled his chair from beneath his desk and sat down. He grabbed a mechanical pencil from his desk drawer and opened his diary. He put on his headphones and took a deep breath.

I don't know how to feel. Some are calling me a hero, some are calling me brave...I don't feel like any of those things. Will my life change now? Will the people at school treat me differently?

Why did Madison risk her life? I treat her so badly...and yet, she continues to support me, to stick up for me. Why? What's in it for her?

Ian shook his head, a frightening thought bubbled to the surface, one that he didn't want to accept. He didn't want Madison to become his friend, because he couldn't stand the pain of losing her...someone that actually liked him for him.

Lastly. What about Peter? Xavier said that it took a thousand years for a ghost to disappear.... Why did Peter vanish? Was it because he did something selfless? Was it because he saved another person's life?

Ian closed his eyes, he could still hear Peter begging, pleading for his help...then when Madison had struck the stalker in the head, and he'd crumpled to the floor—that look on Peter's face when he knew Melody was going to be okay—he disappeared.

Ian turned to a new page in his journal.

I believe, I have found my purpose...I don't know what I am supposed to do, or how to do it yet, but I know that I've been given this...'gift' for a reason.

Ian thought for a moment, and then closed his diary. Right now, he just needed to think. He slowly stood and walked over to his bed.

He heard a soft rap on his door frame. It was Madison. She smiled at him, "May I come in? I wanted to drop off your homework."

"Sure," smiled Ian, actually happy to see her.

"Cue the disco lights," yelled Xavier, "it's his love muffin!"

"Are, your, um…acquaintances here as well?"

Ian looked around the room. Xavier was thrusting his hips, and throwing his fist into the air. Helga was shaking everything she could shake, and Felix was doing the worm on the floor, up the wall, and across the ceiling. "Yes, they're here," Ian said shaking his head.

"What are they doing?" Madison asked, she turned, in a circle, wishing she could see what Ian could see.

"Poetry," Ian smiled, "they're reciting poetry."

We hope you enjoyed reading the first book in The Ghosts of Ian Stanley series. Please leave a review on Amazon, Goodreads, or Barnes & Noble. We'd love to hear from you! Thank you so much for reading our book!

Learn about new book releases by signing up at twistedkeypublishing.com.

Be sure to check out our other exciting books.

Quest Chasers series

Book 1: The Deadly Cavern

Book 2: The Screaming Mummy

Others by Thomas Lockhaven

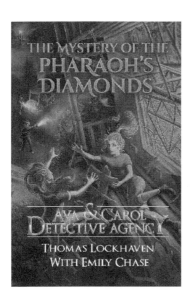

THE HAUNTED MANSION
AVA & CAROL DETECTIVE AGENCY
THOMAS LOCKHAVEN
WITH EMILY CHASE

DOGNAPPED
AVA & CAROL DETECTIVE AGENCY
THOMAS LOCKHAVEN
WITH EMILY CHASE

THE EYE OF GOD
AVA & CAROL DETECTIVE AGENCY
THOMAS LOCKHAVEN

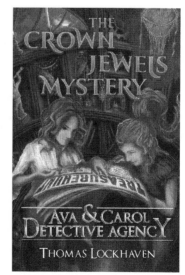

THE CROWN JEWELS MYSTERY
AVA & CAROL DETECTIVE AGENCY
THOMAS LOCKHAVEN

Upcoming title

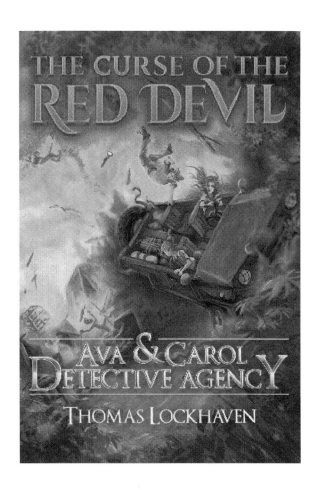

Love adult cozy mysteries?

Check out T. Lockhaven's new series The Coffee House
Sleuths: Sleighed (Book 1)

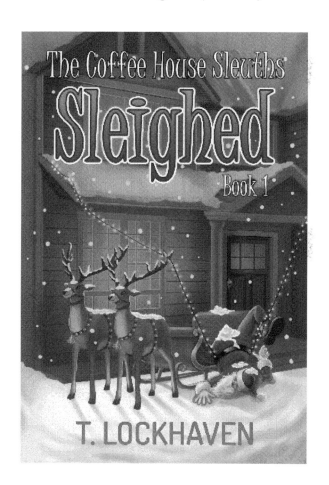

Printed in Great Britain
by Amazon